LEGIONNAIRE FROM TEXAS

Sometimes a serving legionnaire will crack under the brutality of life in a desolate waste and then desert. But the big Texan plans to desert for his own reasons. Why has he joined the foreign legion under an assumed name? And why has an American newspaperwoman, disguised as an Arab girl, joined a caravan crossing the Sahara? When they meet and discover they both share the same secret agenda, they are unaware of their impending life and death struggle to survive . . .

Books by Gordon Landsborough in the Linford Mystery Library:

POISON IVY
FEDERAL AGENT
CALL IN THE FEDS!
F.B.I. SPECIAL AGENT
DEATH SMELLS OF CORDITE
F.B.I. SHOWDOWN
MAKE IT NYLONS
FORTRESS EL ZEEB

GORDON LANDSBOROUGH

LEGIONNAIRE FROM TEXAS

Complete and Unabridged

LINFORD
Leicester

First published in Great Britain

First Linford Edition
published 2012

British Library CIP Data

Landsborough, Gordon.
  Legionnaire from Texas. - -
(Linford mystery library)
  1. Suspense fiction.
  2. Large type books.
  I. Title II. Series
  823.9'14–dc23

  ISBN 978–1–4448–1078–3

Published by
F. A. Thorpe (Publishing)
Anstey, Leicestershire

Set by Words & Graphics Ltd.
Anstey, Leicestershire
Printed and bound in Great Britain by
T. J. International Ltd., Padstow, Cornwall

This book is printed on acid-free paper

1

The narrowed, grey eyes tired of watching after a while and dropped to the sand six inches below them. An ant was scurrying busily, moving in its own shadow because the Sahara sun was directly overhead.

The grey eyes watched it as it came to the perimeter of a smooth little depression. A big, booted foot almost trod the life out of it and the American's hand shot out and grabbed the black-gaitered leg and restrained the movement.

The owner of the foot said, 'What — ?' and looked down. At that moment the ant reached the middle of the tiny hollow in the sand. Suddenly there was a minor convulsion and the ant disappeared.

The American with the cool, grey eyes looked up from the desert sand. Above him was another blue-tunicked Legionnaire.

The American said softly, 'You saw that?' His lean, brown, muscular hand gestured towards the tiny depression that was now devoid of life.

'Yeah, yeah, I saw that.' This was another American, but dark where the recumbent man was fair, brown-eyed where the other was grey. And his voice didn't drawl, it spat words as though his mouth was full of rivets — hot ones.

'Yeah, one moment there was an ant. Next . . . he ain't there. He ain't nowhere.' The brown eyes in the pug face looked puzzled.

Both stared at the little hollow. When you were in the Legion anything that occupied the mind was something to hold on to, even on a hell-march like this.

The lean, rangy American pulled himself on to his side. He was looking again at Ca-ca, the Frenchman who had been a renegade to his country. Ca-ca had caught the bug now and was furtively searching the desert. That made half-a-dozen of them, the American was thinking cynically. Four hours of marching under the pitiless, near-tropical sun, with a kit that weighed as much as the man himself, in many cases. Yet here were six Legionnaires wasting their brief halting space to move about the desert, their eyes searching . . .

'Like a fellar lookin' fer a silver Texas dollar,' the American thought, and then tried to switch his thoughts hurriedly, because he didn't want to be reminded of Texas any more.

His eyes looked again at that tiny, cup-sized depression. He said, 'Elegant, that's like the blamed Foreign Legion, I guess. They bring you out among a lot of sand, an' before you know what's happenin' it's darned well swallowed you up.'

His lean forefinger prodded experimentally under the depression. His companion looked peeved. 'You goldarned Texan,' he yapped. 'You quit callin' me Elegant. The hell, you give me a cissy name like that an' it'll stick.'

Then he stopped griping. Something had come up on the end of that brown finger. Elegant said at once, 'Jeepers, ain't he some louse! Ain't he just the grandfather an' grandmother of all louses!'

It had the same grey, bulbous body, only no louse ever attained its half-inch length.

The grey-eyed American drawled, 'It's an ant-lion, bub. They lurk under the sand, an' when an ant walks above it — '

'You don't need to tell me, brudder.' Elegant had the quick impatience of a Latin, for all his Brooklyn accent. 'Didn't I see it, too?' He brooded over the unpleasant-looking ant-lion. 'Guess I don't ever wanna be an ant with them things around.'

The Texan let the creature drop to the hot sand. In a flash it had burrowed its way out of sight. Elegant started to say, 'There's a lot in this desert I don't like, but most go aroun' on two legs only.'

He let his hot, impatient eyes drift down to where the N.C.O.s were grouped, their kits off so as to refresh them as much as possible during this halt. But the men weren't allowed to take theirs off. It might encourage them in the belief that discipline was at ease, now that the garrison of Sidi-bel-Illah was behind, as their Captain had informed them. They would rest for half an hour wearing their equipment as a reminder that discipline never eased in the French

4

Foreign Legion, he had told them with a smile. He had added also that he felt little fatigue himself, though he had come just as far as they had.

Which was true, though he had omitted two important details. The first was that an officer never carried equipment. The second, he had a horse to save his legs.

The Texan looked across at the dapper little captain his eyes as always, lingering on the revolver in its polished leather holster about the captain's waist. He thought again as he so often thought, 'That's what I need.'

Even a revolver that hadn't been made by Samuel C. Colt. He sighed, and his hands smoothed where once two guns had slapped his thighs. He felt undressed without them even after all this time.

Then his eye caught a too-sudden movement across where Ca-ca had been. Only it wasn't the renegade, but one who was of a kind. Jacques Quelclos who was only half a man's height and didn't like the world because it hadn't supplied him with those extra inches.

Jacques had gone down on one knee,

his eyes staring at the sand before him as if fascinated. Ca-ca and two others came up quickly, said something swiftly to the dwarf man and then all went down on their knees beside Jacques. Then all turned, trying to make their movements casual, and looked down to where the N.C.O.s sprawled and chatted in comfort — or as much comfort as the desert would allow them.

The Texan came upright, though he did it slowly, because of the weight on his back. Elegant started to speak; he hadn't noticed what had attracted the quick attention of his companion. His tone was furtive, too.

'Tex, the boys said for me to come an' talk to you.'

The Texan promptly demanded, 'What boys? The Greek? Kuskov the Russian?' But his eyes never left that little furtive group ahead of him. There was something in that sand that fascinated them, but the distance was too great for the Texan to see what.

The Texan could only see that they were whispering together, and nudging each other as if to egg each other on. Then Ca-ca, who had courage for all that he had worked for the enemy in the big European war — or so it was whispered — Ca-ca did something quickly, something that concerned the sand before him.

The Texan's eyes were almost narrowed out of existence in puzzlement. He didn't understand.

Elegant was talking out of the side of his mouth, his flat, battered features suspiciously watching the hated N.C.O.s. 'It ain't the Greek, an' it ain't that crazy Russian. I don't go nowhere with them guys now. The boys I mean are Louie the Camel, Dimmy, an' the Schemer.'

An All-American side, was Texas' first thought. He was still watching the furtive group across on the sloping side of the sandhill. Albert Cheauvin, who was known as The Weeper, had taken a tobacco tin out of his pack and was emptying it. When it was done he handed it to Ca-ca, whose quick, jerky little movements testified to an almost ungovernable impatience.

'What d'you want me to talk about?'

the rangy Texan who had been a cattle wrangler demanded, his eyes sweeping round suspiciously to the sallow, battered face of the Legionnaire who ill-deserved the name of Elegant. He was shrewd. that ex-cowboy. He whispered, 'You fellars goin' on pump?' . . . deserting. The most serious crime in the French Foreign Legion.

Elegant licked dry lips, and his quick, brown eyes darted from man to man around him, as if to see who was listening, and, if they were too far to hear, who could lip-read from that distance. Then he was reassured. They were all too concerned with snatching a rest to be heeding this whispering pair.

Even Ca-ca and his followers had separated and were lying now on their weighty packs.

'Yeah.' There was grim determination on the Brooklyn boy's face; his eyes were desperate. 'We're gonna be *poumpists* just as soon as we can.' His hand came out urgently, pleadingly, gripping the coarse, blue sleeve of the Texan. 'Brudder, this army ain't fer me. It ain't fer any

American,' he said vigorously.

'Then why'n heck did you join?' *Le Legionnaire Texas* hadn't missed the quick change of hands of that tobacco tin. It was in Ca-ca's pouch now. He was trying to work things out, but could get only halfway, yet he had a feeling of danger as a result of that mystifying little scene on the sandhill.

Elegant scrubbed the beginnings of a beard with black-rimmed fingernails. He avoided the Texan's question.

'Another spell in El Kwatra fort'll send me *fou . . . cafard . . .* screwy. If it's the last thing I do, I'm goin' on pump.'

'I don't like the company you've chosen.' There was a stir down the lines. A brass-lunged voice had shouted. Everyone knew what that meant. A sigh rose from those two hundred men, resting on the yielding, hot sand of the Sahara. It was hell to lie there in the pitiless heat of that blazing fiery orb, but another four hours of marching would make that hell a heaven by comparison.

They stirred, those men, groaning and cursing, turning on all fours before

9

attempting to rise to their feet, because with that weight on their backs, it was the only way they could get upright.

Elegant looked up anxiously into the face of the tall Texan. 'What d'you need me for?' said Texas. The scouts who had been posted distantly to watch for hostile Arab forces were trudging in now on all sides.

Elegant sighed. There was something like admiration on his tough, young face — respect, anyway. Everyone respected this slow-drawling, good-humoured Texan who didn't fit into the Legion because clearly he wasn't an outcast of any country. Everyone knew this ex-cowpuncher hadn't failed so much in life that he must seek oblivion in the hardest, most merciless army on earth. And men whispered, thinking about this difference between themselves and the American, and wondered what had brought him into their ranks.

It wasn't as if he looked the kind to make a fool of himself over a woman — more likely the other way, they decided looking at that lean, muscular seventy-five inches of sun-bronzed manhood. *Le*

Legionnaire Texas was a man's man and a woman's too . . .

'Tex, you ol' maverick, you got somep'n we want. Experience.' They were forming into line now, four deep, Elegant was whispering urgently, desperate now to win the Texan to their side.

'What you don't know about deserts ain't worth knowin'. You've lived in 'em all your life — '

'Texan an' Mexican deserts, not this dog-blasted heap.'

Elegant lifted hands that were fringed with frayed tunic. Elegant didn't well describe him; in an army of inelegant men, the Brooklyn boy was the least prepossessing. The gesture said, 'What the heck's the difference?' The mouth phrased it differently. 'Ain't it all just a lot of sand? I ain't never seen a desert that wasn't. An' you c'n live in a desert, Tex, where we guys'd go under. You got the know-how, an' we need you.'

Tex waited until he was sure that the lean-faced, black-eyed Frenchman who had no other name in the Legion but Ca-ca was coming to his side. Then he

11

whispered sidelong, 'I don't like the company you keep, pard. Sure as hell, you'll all land in the *cellules*. That or roastin' over an Arab fire. Include me out, brother . . . '

Elegant looked before him as *le Capitaine* came riding up on a white horse so big for the little man that he could have made a bed on its back and not fallen off at a gallop. The sergeants were stamping and bellowing as he came nearer.

Ca-ca was relaxed and unsuspecting by his side. The Legionnaire from Texas turned those cool, grey eyes upon the renegade and said in what passed for French in the Legion, 'I figger there's only two things live under sand, *mon petit*,' The Frenchman went stiff at the words, and it seemed that the colour drained from his sallow cheeks. His head came slowly round, so that eyes, widened with shock, could stare into the face of the drawling American.

'Yeah, two things. One's an ant-lion, but they don't hurt anythin' save ants.' The Texan continued that long look.

He knew this renegade was up to something, just as he had first suspected. Something very deep and dirty, or it wouldn't be Ca-ca, of course.

'I figger you ain't got no interest in ants, so I reckon I know what's in that tin box o' yourn — the one you got from The Weeper.' He was curious. He wanted to know what use a Legionnaire could have for such a thing . . .

That big white horse was almost on top of them, the little, prinked-up dandy of an officer comfortably perched on the glossy saddle. Texas got his eyes to the front, because the officer could be vicious or sarcastic, and *le Legionnaire Texas* didn't enjoy either from the man.

Suddenly the life went out of his legs. He felt a sharp blow, cunningly dealt to the base of his spine. Afterwards he decided it was from the haft of a knife. Texas crashed face downwards on to the hot, yielding sand, his fall aided and accelerated by the weight on his back.

A startled, white horse reared, and the Legionnaire had a vision of flailing hoofs beating the air and about to descend on him. If one of those sharp hooves hit his skull . . .

He tried to roll away, but found the paralysis still held.

He was helpless, unable to move, and those hooves were crashing down towards him . . .

Elegant grabbed him by the legs and yanked, and over six-foot of Texan was dragged out of danger. Then strength returned to the Texan; all at once the paralysis that had followed that nerve-shattering blow left him. He was able to rise to his feet, to draw himself erect, and look into the impassive face of Ca-ca, the man who had a secret.

The Captain was shouting, fighting to bring his startled mount under control. He was a little man, not a good officer because he had a contempt for his men, but he could ride a horse like a professional jockey. Within seconds he had the sweating, trembling beast passive once more.

The *Chef* came riding up then, raging behind his two gold chevrons that such a thing should happen on a parade conducted by him. *Ma foi*, what was the meaning of this, when a soldier couldn't stand on the legs *le Bon Dieu* had supplied him with? The sergeant-major was bellowing as only the sergeant-major could bellow. His sergeants came running up to support him, and they, too, were shouting and seeming very angry . . . it paid, in the French Foreign Legion, to shout and seem very angry when *le Capitaine* was around. Promotion, it was said, was always given to the loudest and the angriest of men.

The *Chef* roared, what in God's name had the American to say for himself? Texas stood in silence. He was experienced in the ways of the Legion, and knew no possible good could come of opening his mouth. There would be punishment enough without that.

He stood at attention, while a storm of sergeants and their sergeant major, a lieutenant, and a captain shouted abuse at him. Not a word did he say about the treacherous blow of Ca-ca, the renegade. His eyes narrowed against the reflecting light of the blazing sun, his lips compressed into a bloodless line — he let the storm rage until the inevitable end.

The American would be given strength to his legs at Fort EI Kwatra, stormed the *Chef*. There would be pack drill in the heat of the day for him — two hours of it, for a week. In one week, the *Chef* promised passionately, there would be such strength in *le Legionnaire Texas* that he would never again fall down on parade. He was an evil man, that *Chef*, delighting in the savagery of the punishments he imposed. Now he was purple in the face as he declared sentence on the Legionnaire.

Up on his white horse, the little Captain listened, good-humoured because, to his way of thinking, the situation was being handled admirably. This Sergeant-major Ransconi was a fine fellow, though another of these blue-chinned Italians who didn't know how to wash. The sentence was just *le Capitaine* agreed. Men must be taught not to fall under the feet of his horse. *Ma foi*, the beast might trip and who was to know a leg wouldn't be broken, and this was a valuable animal.

In time the hubbub died, the line was straightened and the order given, '*En avant! Marche!*'

Ca-ca was in front of Texas now. Deliberately Tex lifted his big shapeless boot and kicked. Ca-ca gasped and staggered while all the men around turned sweating, dust-covered faces in surprise. Never before had they seen the Texan in such a mood.

Then Ca-ca heard the drawling voice behind him. 'That's for a start *amigo*. You've got a lot comin' to you, but it'll come later.'

*   *   *

Eight hours and twenty-two miles later, they halted for the last time before reaching the Legion post known as Fort El Kwatra. Where they stopped was just another rolling plain of yellow sand, but now the dunes threw long shadows — long enough to hide an army of ambushing Arabs, as every Legionnaire there knew.

In three more hours they would march

upon the fortress whose garrison they were to relieve for the next three months. Three hours, they quoth, and then they would know the meaning of hell. Three months in this desert outpost would send a good half of them with the crawling beetle of *cafard* in their brains. The fact that not all these would run amok and die was because by that time they would be without the strength of mind either to kill themselves or take the mad risk of desertion.

Elegant was squatting by Texas's head. He was arguing, doing his best to persuade the big fellow to join them.

'You know what it was like last time. Tex, we'll be gettin' to fightin' all the time after a coupla weeks. Rube says, 'why not make a dash for it while we've got strength'?'

'The Schemer?' Tex's back was sore where that blow had struck him, but he had recovered his customary good humour by now. 'Him, he's always sayin' things. He gets the screwiest ideas.'

The worst of Rube Koskowsci, he'd been a peddler of insurance back in the

States, and he could get most men to listen to his schemes.

'Maybe he's not so screwy, Tex.' Elegant fastened another yielding button with a thin piece of wire. He was the most patched-up man in a regiment of patched-up men.

Tex's eyes followed Ca-ca. The Frenchman had hurriedly left Tex's side at the cry of '*Halte!*' Now he was with his cronies. The Weeper, Dwarf Quelclos who fought a man as soon as look at him, and Mervin Petrie, who had been an assistant at the Marseilles guillotine until he qualified for a more central role himself and gladly joined the Legion. The Bulgar was there, too, with his bad teeth and surly ill-humour, and last of all was La Femme.

He was the worst of the lot, Tex always thought. For he was as pretty as a girl, but so corrupt and evil underneath it didn't seem possible that those blue eyes could hold the innocence they did. And La Femme was a bully, only he was worse than most bullies.

He was a bully of women.

19

Elegant's battered face grew intense as he strove for words to interest his companion. 'He's got a head, that Schemer. The guy's got it all figured out. Every *poumpist* travels north to get to a port an' they always get picked up. Now the Schemer, he says 'The hell, we'll go south. It's longer, but it's safer'.'

'South?' The Texan wrinkled his nose. 'Goin' south sure brings you nowhere but the middle of Africa.'

Elegant shook his head in triumph. He wasn't usually very fast with his head-piece, and it did him good to feel he was one up on the rangy Texan.

'The Schemer says, 'That's what they all think. That's why they all strike nort' fer the coast, an' so the Military Police never need to move away from the ports because in time, the *poumpists* just walk into their hands.'

'Nope. The Schemer says, 'We'll head souf'. When we get to Lake Chad we'll be safe in British Territory', What d'you say, Tex?'

Tex said it again, good-humouredly for all his terseness. 'The Schemer's nuts,

Elegant, I tell you. He ain't a bad fellar, mind you, but he kinda gets taken away by his own spiel. But the fellar you wanna watch, brother, is that Louie the Camel . . . '

'Aw, Louie ain't bad.' The flat, battered Brooklyn face wrinkled into a disclaimer. 'He gets kinda touchy about many things, but I reckon he'll pass. Now, Tex, for the last time — '

Tex saw activity in that little group ahead of him and started to lurch clumsily to his feet. He snapped, 'The answer's still no, Bird-brain. Lake Chad's all of fifteen hundred miles from here — '

'There's a caravan route all the way, the Schemer says.' Elegant was climbing up alongside the ex-puncher, pleading.

The Texan said, contemptuously, 'The Schemer says!' And they were on the edge of the group, just as a man screamed.

It was Ca-ca.

He was pirouetting on his heels in agony, his face flung back to the evening sky, his mouth wide and screaming the scream of a man who sees nothing but death ahead for him. His companions had

21

split up, pulling away suddenly, as if in fright of what they saw in their midst.

Men were lurching to their feet, some gripping their Lebels because this could be the prelude to an evening attack by the Arabs who always knew when a relief column was being sent to El Kwatra. The officers were taking to their horses; Sergeant-Major Ransconi was bellowing his head off with rage immediately; and sergeants and corporals were milling around, trying to find out where the noise originated from.

Texas halted no more than a dozen yards from the raving Ca-Ca. He saw froth bubbling from that screaming mouth. Then Ca-ca went plunging away into the desert just as the scouts on their western flank were shot down by Arabs who had crawled near to them because they had cleverly used the dying sun as a blinding background to their movements.

Texas thought for one moment that he saw a look of astonishment on Ca-ca's face before he went reeling away into the evening shadows that were long and purple and could enfold a man within minutes.

2

All in seconds those spectators took in the scene. The dying sun, and the men. rolling down that long, wind-rippled dune a quarter of a mile to the west of them. Ca-ca staggering away screaming, and no one knew why. No one, that is, except the furtive, frightened quintet who were still pushing and milling around where they had been quietly whispering a half-moment before.

But Texas was guessing. As the *Chef* rode up, his mind diverted between this incident and the tumbling corpses on that sandy hillside, he plunged forward.

Something was wriggling, on the silky sand that was as fine as sifted pepper, hereabouts. Something little thicker than a pencil, and not much longer.

Texas saw the lemon-grey shape writhe until it was just under the surface, and then become immediately still, its position marked though, by a ridge that outlined its frightened body.

The Weeper was pointing, and shouting, 'Ca-ca is a dead 'un. That thing bit Ca-ca while he rested.'

Texas's head swung round.

Ca-ca hadn't been resting.

The *Chef* shouted, '*Retournez!*' but Ca-ca wouldn't turn — couldn't turn. He seemed to go forward on to his face in the shadows and lie there and writhe for seconds and then twitch into gradual stillness. The *Chef* swore, his face evil with passion that a man should get out of the Legion so lightly just when he was needed to fight these accursed *Afriques*!

'He is a pig and a fool,' he shouted, raging. 'Only a pig and a fool would rest on top of a sand viper.' Then he turned his horse's head, spurring and sending it plunging to where the officers were mounting and shouting to their men to take up battle formation.

Mervin Petrie stamped upon the sand viper where it lay coiled a half-inch deep below the surface. Perhaps it was appropriate that he should do the executioner's work upon the murderer of their comrade. The thing, dying, lashed its way to the surface. Tex, stumbling over to join the kneeling line of men, saw the satisfaction on the Marseilles executioner's face.

He saw the feminine features of La Femme wrinkle with disgust, and The Weeper was weeping from that left eye of his, and Quelclos was snarling as if things had gone wrong somewhere.

But the Bulgar, who was unsubtle, stumbled by and it seemed to Tex that he was satisfied about something . . . He remembered that bad-toothed, half-grin later.

It was the usual attack by the usual crowd of Arabs. For the past year every relieving force that had come to the fort had been attacked by waiting Arabs. The tactics were puzzling. Some local sheik must have been trying to win honour, but his force, though numerically superior, was badly armed; and each time had been beaten off.

The only trouble was, each time the attacks grew more severe — each time the Arab sheik seemed to call upon a larger force that was more difficult to beat off. Reports that had come through to Sidi-bel-Illah on the coast spoke of gathering of tribes and a restlessness throughout the land that could only end in a major flare-up.

Ca-ca, lying out there in the shadows, was forgotten. The men knelt in a long crescent where they had halted, their Lebels pointing, their fingers ready. Tex had naturally taken his place alongside his American comrades; and there was the Legionnaire who wasn't elegant, snapping Brooklyn wisecracks out of the corner of his mouth, and Louie the Camel snarling back; Dimmy Dimicci wasn't thinking but would react the moment the order came through to fire — and Rube Koskowsci, Polish-born American, was nimbly thinking up a scheme in case these damn' Arabs captured him.

The Arabs had crested the brow to the west of them. There were three or four hundred white-robed figures, sitting their horses as if they were part of them. They were milling around, kicking up a lot of dust, and the waiting Legionnaires could hear their excited cries.

They always made the same mistakes, these Arabs, thought Texas, squinting down the barrel of his Lebel. They should have come charging in with their first shots, instead of which they were pep-talking each other into a charge that would be fatal to so many. In a moment, though, they would come raging and screaming down upon the infidels who had come to occupy their lands. They would fight recklessly, gallantly, and then the Lebels would empty too many saddles and they would have to pull away.

Now, if ever these Arabs got their hands on a few hundred Lebels — even more, upon a machine-gun or two . . .

Sergeant-Major Ransconsi came riding behind them. He was calling them his children. He was a brave man, though a brute who should never have lived, and he was indifferent to his exposed position up there on his black Arab stallion.

'*Mes enfants*, you are children of France. You will fight — indeed you will fight. Today you will bring glory to the tricolour and will teach these savages the effrontery of attacking the glorious Legion.'

'Savages?' Texas spat the word upon the sandy soil. Were they not savages, too, these mercenaries of the Legion? He a citizen of the State of Texas, could not be expected to understand things in the way they did in Europe.

The mass of mounted figures was separating, straightening into a long line. Now, at some word of command unheard by the tense soldiers of the Legion, the Arabs began their charge. Failing light gleamed redly on sword and scimitar, dagger and gun barrel, though the guns were few enough and were probably anything up to a hundred years old.

Screaming their war cry, the Arabs made their charge upon the accursed Franks whom they regarded as responsible for the ills and discomforts of their existence.

'*Allah-o-akbar!*'

The cry rose in a ragged wave of sound from hundreds of savage throats. With that cry on their lips, they were prepared to ride to death; for did not death at the hands of the infidel only serve to qualify them for eternal existence in the hereafter?

A sharp word of command tightened every finger on those rock-steady Lebels. Eyes squinted but saw straight and true. In a flurry of dust that was a miniature sandstorm, rising higher than the *kafir* of the riders, the charge thundered up to the long, blue crescent.

Tex had time to think, 'This is gonna be somethin' tough!' It would take all their time to repel this charge — truly the Arab attacks were becoming more formidable. Then the Captain's voice rang above the screaming noise of the attackers — 'Fire!'

A mighty crashing roar echoed and re-echoed down the line. Smoke rose as shoulders jarred. Two hundred arms moved like pistons, ejecting the spent cartridges and inserting fresh ones. Saddles were suddenly, miraculously, swept clear of riders, so that horses ran wildly across the heads of their laden fellows, often bringing them to grief.

As the smoke cleared, it was seen that

there was panic and pandemonium on the right flank of the attackers, but the centre and left horn of the attacking crescent was still coming on.

Captain Duvet made his big mistake then. His trouble was that he was too contemptuous of all save those who were born to the rank of gentleman, and later, officer. Sitting his white horse behind the centre of his infantry, he saw the Arab right wing wilt and crumple and fade away before one salvo of shot, and he thought, 'Another and these *sales cochons* will all turn and flee,' and he held on to the word 'Fire!' too long.

He let the flood of Arabs come almost within bayoneting distance before his confident voice sang out a second time, 'Fire!'

The howling, blood-maddened Arabs were in among the ranks in the centre before the roar of firing had died, before the smoke of those death-dealing Lebels had chance to clear.

A sergeant thundered the order, 'A bayonet!' And then went down as an Arab *flissa* hacked murderously at him.

Tex and the Americans instinctively sprang together, forgetting the weight of their encumbering packs in that moment of near death for them all. Around them horses plunged, many whinnying with fear some screaming with pain. Swarthy, lean-featured Arabs bent from their saddles and hacked with cutting weapons, teeth gleaming in the last rays of daylight as they shouted their war cries.

There was a brief, savage moment of stab, parry and then bludgeon with the butt. Dust rose as the trampling mass swayed to the weight of battle. There was constant noise, the sound of men's voices lifted in wild passion as they strove to kill because otherwise they would be killed. Shots occasionally, and the crash of steel upon steel. Men fell, wounded, to crawl away. Others fell — and never moved again.

Texas swung his rifle. His height helped against the mounted Arabs. Elegant and the others were being pressed by two horsemen who were rearing right over the top of them. That swinging butt of the ex-cowboy emptied one saddle and then he nearly knocked the other black-bearded rider to the ground.

Another rider came crashing through, and Texas was sent flying. When he got to his knees he found himself behind his savagely fighting comrades, intent on saving him from the lance or sword. He found his Lebel and went plunging back into the fray. He realized there was blood on his face, but couldn't remember the blow that had started it.

Then the attack pulled away. Only in the centre, where the charge had been closest when the captain's belated order to fire had rung out — only there had the fighting become hand to hand. Now the victorious Legionnaires on either flank were pumping lead into the supporting wave of Arabs who were racing in to help their comrades at grips with the Franks. It turned them, and having no support, the first wave pulled away and raced into the gloom of gathering night for safety.

Several failed to make it, however. One was an Arab who had to fight his way past the tiny group of American Legionnaires to get his freedom. Texas saw a flailing scimitar. Ducked and in the same movement caught the booted foot and hurled the rider out of the saddle.

The white-robed Arab crashed to the ground. Instantly half a dozen Legionnaires were there, bayonets seeking that body.

But Le Legionnaire Texas was there before them. He was standing astride the stunned Arab, his Lebel with its wicked gleaming bayonet pointing . . . and pointing at Legionnaires this time, not Arabs.

'Hold back,' gasped the big Texan. 'This fellar's my prisoner.'

He didn't know why he did it. In the heat of the battle it was to be expected that a man killed whenever he had the opportunity. But some instinct made the Texan intervene.

Stooping, he hoisted the Arab on to his feet. He could hardly see the face, because the light was bad now to the point of being almost non-existent, but he had an impression of more-than-ordinary prisoner. This was an Arab of some rank.

There weren't many prisoners. The way

of the Legion was to leave no wounded to the enemy, yet in some way four Arabs, including Tex's prisoner, had been captured.

Elegant growled, 'If you thought you were bein' kind, Tex, you made a big mistake then. That guy's gonna suffer — an' still die.'

Tex, getting back into line and searching the night for an attacking enemy, didn't answer. In his heart he knew his companion was right.

There would be brutal treatment for the prisoners right until the time they were tried by a military court. Men like Sergeant-Major Ransconsi the Italian, would have their pleasure on the men, and then they would doubtless be shot out of hand.

Tex thought, 'Maybe it's better not to try to be kind.' And then the order to reform and recommence the march was given. The badly wounded were put on stretchers and borne by their comrades as the little force plunged into the darkness of the desert night.

But the march lasted only an hour.

Captain Duvet had intended to reach the fortress by about midnight, but even so they would have to camp outside the walls because El Kwatra wouldn't hold both them and the present garrison. The captain therefore graciously called a halt and ordered camp for the night to be made less than five miles from their destination.

He explained that it was out of concern for the wounded, and the men knew he spoke the truth but knew it was for a reason other than the one he gave.

Captain Anton Duvet had a small enough force indeed to patrol the desert and guard Fort El Kwatra for the next three months without seeing many wounded die on his hands this night. No; far better to patch them up so that they could hold a rifle again if needed. When they got back to the garrison at Sidi-bel-Illah, then they could die, he thought cheerfully. There were many such scum as these to take their place for the next tour of duty . . .

Fires were lit, because the enemy had had a severe beating that evening and weren't expected to return. *Soupe*, gristly with old horseflesh, and hunks of coarse brown bread were served; then, wrapped in *capote* and brown issue blanket, the exhausted men fell asleep.

From the time of capturing him until the moment he was wakened to go on guard, Tex never gave another thought to his prisoner; but in the four hours in the middle of the night that constituted his watch, he couldn't help thinking about him, if only because he was detailed to stand guard over him.

The four Arabs had been tied and thrown down near to a fire. A special guard of four men and a corporal had been detailed to guard them, and Tex was on this duty.

He stood on the edge of the firelight, his eyes never leaving the prisoners. The three other guards stood around, watching just as vigilantly.

After a while Tex realized two things. One was that the Arab he had captured wasn't sleeping at all but was watching him through half-closed eyes; the other — *none of the Arabs was tied!*

36

In some miraculous way one of them must have got his wrists free of the cruelly tight, camel-hair ropes, and no doubt he had slipped a hidden knife through the bonds of his comrades and released them, too.

It was on the tip of Tex's tongue to shout a warning, and then he became silent. After all, he shrugged, what did it matter to him. If these Arabs escaped, what harm would it do to anyone — even France? But if they died, and it became known how they died, it would only bring the never-ceasing desert war into a phase of greater savagery. It always happened.

Indifferently he thought, 'It doesn't matter a damn. Let 'em get away — if they can.'

Shortly before the end of his watch, though, he began to realize that for all they had released themselves from their bonds, these Arabs were still just as much prisoners as before. They were seeking a moment of inattention on the part of their guards, but Tex knew it would never come.

He began to study the face of the man

he had caught and made prisoner. He tried to feel the despair that gripped the man, as night rolled swiftly by and dawn crept up to the eastern skyline. Once daylight came, these men wouldn't stand a chance of escaping.

He was only young, for all his pointed black beard, and now, with frustration gnawing at him, his brown eyes were big and wide and shining. Perhaps because there was no one else to look at, they never looked away from the big, silent Legionnaire from Texas, and after a time it became uncomfortable for the American — in time it almost seemed to him that the Arab by that red-glowing fire of dried camel dung was appealing to him, his captor.

Tex just stood, apparently immovable, resting on his rifle, but he was thinking. There was pity in the big man's heart. This was only a kid, for all the trappings of the Arab warrior. A youth for all his black, pointed beard. He was going to suffer a lot in the next days until his inevitable death against a mud wall at the hands of a firing-party.

Tex stirred, thinking of the suffering that was to come to this Arab. He'd seen them roughly, brutally handled before, and, a free-born American, he hadn't liked it.

He thought, 'Yeah, the fellar's gotta go through the hoop an' I'm the guy responsible for it all.' Better that he had let his comrades kill the Arab out of hand . . .

When he was relieved and began to trudge away from the now dull-glowing fire, it seemed to Tex that the Arab turned his *kaffired* head to watch after him. As if the man had known the thoughts of compassion in the big American's mind, and was silently appealing for succour.

Other guards were coming in through the paling dawn as Tex strode across to where his kit was stacked. The Camel hadn't been on, and was sleeping by a fire. Tex could see his open mouth and unshaven, sunken cheeks as he snored. Another quarter of an hour, he thought, and dawn would be upon them — and then the Arabs wouldn't stand a chance of escape.

Le Legionnaire Ellighan came drooping across and stacked his rifle, and then came Dimmy Dimicci, who was so dumb that he didn't always answer to his own name. Rube Koskowsci, The Schemer because of his inventive mind, showed up as the three men stretched for a final brief rest on the soft sand. He looked as fresh and alert as ever, red-cheeked and bright-eyed and seemingly untouched by fatigue.

Tex looked at him and was satisfied. Then he lay on his back and looked at the stars that were fading before the growing light, and his voice drawled, softly so that only his American comrades could hear him, 'Them Ay-rabs has gotten their mitts free.'

Elegant scratched his leg through a hole in his white trousers and yawned, 'So what? I couldn't care what happened to them guys.'

Tex looked at those stars and said, 'That don't make 'em free, though. An' ef they can't figger out a way of escape afore daylight, I reckon they'll never get chance to escape agen.' Within a few hours they would be inside Fort El Kwatra. Deliberately he pulled the strings of sentiment. 'One's only a kid, for all he's grown a beard. Looks no older than Rube.'

He knew The Schemer was listening, because the young Polish-American hadn't got down on the sand alongside them. All this would be as a challenge to Rube's fertile imagination, as the Texan well knew.

The man from Texas sighed. 'Now, if only someone had brains enough to figger up a distraction — somethin' to get the eyes of that guard off'n the prisoners for a moment . . . '

He didn't finish his sentence. He didn't need to. He caught the crunch of sand as a man's weight stood on it as he would in rising. Tex rolled on to his side and saw a shadow steal away towards the guard fire, no more than forty yards away.

After that he saw nothing — only a sudden spiral of sparks from the near-dead fire, as if something had been thrown on it. Someone shouted at that, possibly the guard corporal. Then the fire blew up.

Not all at once. There was a crack as of

41

a rifle round exploding, and some of the fire showered out. Then came a whole succession of crackling sounds, as if a whole bunch of rounds went crashing off together, and more fire cascaded over a range of ten or twenty yards. Then there was a miniature explosion and quite a lot of red embers shot on to the blankets of the nearby, sleeping Legionnaires.

As a distraction it was perfect. Legionnaires awoke from sleep to find their blankets beginning to set on fire — and their howls built up to a pandemonium of sound. The guard, meanwhile, had promptly started blazing off at some suspected movement away from the camp.

Tex grinned comfortably and continued to lie where he was. Rest was the best thing; only fools ran about when they knew there was nothing to run about for. And Tex and one other knew there was nothing to fear in spite of all the hullabaloo that raged over the camp.

That other came in quietly, a few seconds later. Tex heard his grunting voice as he came sidling in like a crab, so as to keep down out of the way of any stray bullets. The light was fairly good now, and the ex-puncher could see the grin of satisfaction on that round, red, boyish face.

The Schemer jumped, startled, as Tex's soft voice asked, 'Did they get away?'

Koskowsci relaxed, relieved. 'Sure,' he whispered. 'Went out like hosses from their stalls at the startin' pistol. Now the guard's firin' like hell so's to make out they were rescued in a raid. That'll get 'em out of trouble; no one'll ever know.'

He was chuckling. He whispered, delighted, to the Texan, 'You know what I did? I slung a pouchful of ammo on to that fire. Thass all. But wasn't it a good scheme, huh?'

Tex whispered back, 'So good, brother, I figger maybe you could get through to Lake Chad, as you say . . . '

★   ★   ★

Forty miles away an Arab camp was stirring to life. The camels were being led out, protesting viciously at being disturbed, their loose underlips trembling to

43

the bubbling, hissing noise that was intimidating to at least one person at that border oasis.

In a black-goatskinned guest tent, a silk-clad *houri* surveyed herself as well as possible by the aid of a small hand mirror. She fitted the soft, clinging gossamer that was the yashmak across the bridge of her short, straight nose and was ready to take the trail.

She looked rather small in her curved-toed slippers, but she looked soft and alluring and lovely. There was grace as she walked about her tent, for all it wasn't the swinging grace of the peasant born to carrying the water jars on her head.

And her eyes were blue as the Sahara sky above. And when she spoke aloud, saying, 'I wonder if I'll see him this trip?' her voice wasn't an Arab's.

It was American.

3

Suddenly, miraculously, springing from nowhere, a group of riders appeared on the wind-ridged sandhills to the north-west of the caravan train. At once arose cries of dejection and despair, and the sound travelled down the long line until it reached the camels upon which travelled the women of the tribe.

At once bejewelled hands reached for the silken hangings of the tent-like compartments in which they travelled, and drew them lest the eye of the infidel see them. Yet their own eyes were to the cracks in the curtains, watching eagerly, for many of these Franks were good to look upon. Especially those god-like men whose hair was as fair as corn in high summer.

The horsemen came galloping easily towards the halting caravan. By the time they reached it, the beasts were already settling on to their haunches, and the whole train had stopped.

By now the desert wanderers knew the ways of the Legion; and knew that all must stop when the blue-soldiers came riding up. The elders muttered in their beards, and their followers looked fierce and talked of smiting the accursed dogs who had no right in Africa, anyway. Yet no one performed a hostile act when the ten soldiers under their N.C.O. rode in among them; for France struck hard when anyone sought to dispute her power.

Instead the sheiks advanced with dignity to meet the Legionnaires and called the blessings of Allah upon them, and if they didn't sound too enthusiastic, then no doubt Allah forgave them for what they had suffered before at the hands of these search parties.

The sergeant in charge of the party gave back a short greeting, then made a terse demand to be permitted to search the caravan. No arms must be carried, he told them; they had enough trouble without Arabs from Tripoli coming over the border to start private feuds of their own. Arms would be confiscated, he called, and when the oldest sheik said, 'By the beard of the Prophet, we carry no arms save a knife or two to cut our food,' the sergeant merely grunted that they would search the caravan for all that.

He and his men dismounted; then, leaving two men in charge of their horses and to cover them in case of trouble, the sergeant led the Legionnaires up to the first camel and began the search.

The sergeant looked through the well-filled packs, carefully tossing the contents on to the sand. The owner looked on, his face a mask to hide the rage that consumed his soul at sight of his precious belongings being so rudely handled.

'Nothing there,' growled the crop-headed sergeant. He picked up a big cake of pressed dates that must have weighed ten kilos and passed it to one of his men to take to the horses. 'We'll take that,' he said with satisfaction. Food was scarce at the post; meeting these caravans helped to supplement the diet.

The elderly Arab who owned the dates involuntarily moved a step forward at that, his hand lifted in protest. The sergeant wheeled, intimidating, his eyes narrowed truculently, challenging.

'Don't you want us to have your so-nice dates?' he sneered. His hand dropped to the bayonet that was in its clumsy metal scabbard. The Arab came to an abrupt halt remembering what happened when these unpleasant soldiers were thwarted. They could trump up all manner of excuses to march them in to that dreaded Fort El Kwatra. Apart from the delay, there was always a fine on top of it, when any caravan was led to the desert post. Even if they didn't carry weapons (which they did, securely hidden from even the most cunning of Legion searchers) the unpleasant Legionnaires would swear to finding some, and that was excuse for the heavy fine that followed.

So now the Arab spread his hands and turned his back until the Legionnaires had gone on to the next camel.

One of the party shoved back his *kepi*, and his hair had that fairness that pleased Arab women, used always to the coarse black hair of their menfolk. He was tall and leanly fit, and looked a man not to be trifled with, for all the air of calm that seemed settled on him.

Now he said, out of the corner of his mouth, 'I figger we're nothin' but a lotta bandits,' and his voice was filled with disgust.

'Sure,' agreed le legionnaire Joe Ellighan. 'We're a bunch o' hijackers, no better, I guess.'

But they had to obey orders, and they went down the line assisting the sergeant in his search of the unfortunate people. By the time they had come towards the end of the train, their horses were laden with booty — fruit and chocolate, dates and food, but also bottles of native wine. The Arabs looked resigned but weren't pleased at having encountered a desert patrol. If they had been luckier, they might have slipped by undetected, and then they would have been the richer by what the greedy Franks were taking from them now.

The sergeant, pleased with his morning's work, opened a bottle of wine and took a long swig. When he had finished he wiped away a trickle of red liquid that ran through the blue stubble of his chin, and then he pointed to the laden camels at the rear.

'Now, *mes arabis*, let us examine those for the arms which undoubtedly you carry somewhere in your train,' he ordered.

That brought the Arabs in an angry, expostulating group about the Legionnaires. They grouped quickly, their Lebels at the ready. The sergeant's eyes narrowed furiously. He was a man trained not to be baulked in his orders.

'What is this?' he shouted. 'Will you stand in my way because I wish to search the camels of your womenfolk? Do you dogs not realize that you are opposing the servants of *la belle France*?'

The dogs did, but still they pressed around in an angry, infuriated mob.

And suddenly *le Legionnaire Texas* got the idea that they were inordinately uneasy. That they were kicking up a bigger fuss than usual when it came to a search of the women's camels. He looked round swiftly, and caught an eye watching him

50

through a parting in the silk curtain of a decorated palanquin on top of an ugly, bad tempered she-camel.

The eye was blue above the *yashmak*, the hair golden under the silken turban of the girl. Dimly silhouetted through the heavy silk curtains, though, he could see her form, and her dress was Arab in style.

The eye continued to look at him. He thought, 'She's purty mad at me . . . all of us.' And he didn't blame the owner.

The sergeant started to bellow to the Arabs to stand back, but they didn't yield. Plainly they were determined to stop the search of their womenfolk's camels if it were at all possible.

The sergeant's shout distracted Tex's attention from the girl and he looked to his front. He saw angry faces, some bearded, some moustached, all long and browned by a life in the sun. Hands were clenched within the folds of their multi-coloured garments, and he knew that it needed little to set some fanatic leaping forward in a death struggle.

While he had learned sympathy for the long-suffering Arabs in his year in the

Legion, he was yet a man who wanted to go on living, and his rifle was up and pointing with the others.

All the same, the sergeant was intimidated. He'd got what he wanted anyway — good food and wine to supplement the awful diet of the fortress. He saw that to insist on the search might bring disaster to his small party, so he suddenly capitulated.

'*Cochons*,' he said graciously, 'I am moved by a natural kindness to allow your womenfolk to pass without search.' And then he added, 'They are, in any event, as sour as vinegar and not to be looked at by men who do not wish to see women who are wrinkled and old and useless. Now take away. '*Allez!*' he roared in fury.

At that the girl in the silken tent on top of the camel sighed and shook her head. 'Not him,' she was thinking. The man she wanted to meet wouldn't have behaved like this sergeant.

The sergeant stood back along with his Legionnaires and roared again to the camel leader to set his train going. There was no need for him to roar, no need for him to give any orders, but it was second nature to an N.C.O. long in the service of the Legion to do both.

Tex, standing next to La Femme, who was watching the womenfolk with a calculating eye, suddenly realised that the sergeant's order was not being obeyed. Not a camel lifted gruntingly to its feet at the behest of its master; not one of the bearded leaders of the caravan shouted for them to be on their way from these accursed thieving infidels.

Every Arab was standing very still. Brown, terrified eyes were looking beyond the group — were looking at something behind the sergeant.

The sergeant shouted passionately again for them to be on their way, and then his words died into the silence of all who stood there. It had dawned on him that there was something unusually wrong, and simultaneously with one of his legionnaires he turned his head to look behind him.

A rifle fell into the dust.

Silently surveying them from a distance

of no more than fifty yards away, from the side of a wind-eroded dune that was nearly pure white sand, was a party of mounted men.

All but one of the dozen were Arabs — or at least they were dressed in the flowing robes of the desert Bedouin. That one wore the uniform of a captain of the Legion under his Arab headdress.

The sergeant looked at those silent, sinister figures on their motionless horses and gasped. They wore nothing that identified them, but somehow what they were was stamped on their appearance ... there was an aura of savagery, of cruelty, of barely controlled viciousness about the group that gave him the clue ...

He exclaimed, shocked and horrified, '*Partizans!*'

Texas recovered his rifle. Never in his life before had he dropped a weapon. His eyes weren't looking at the *partizans*, though — they were on that captain ...

At the word *partizans* the rest of the Legionnaires, including the careless one with the horses, who should have been keeping better watch but had thought the enemy to be within the caravan, all came wheeling round.

At once the glinting barrels of Lebels rose from under the robes of those silent *partizans* to cover the Legionnaires. The soldiers were at the mercy of this sinister group, but the Arabs with the camel train didn't seem any more pleased at the tables being turned on them. Instead they looked as if they would have preferred their former insolent masters.

'*Partizans!*' gasped the rest of the Legionnaires. all except Dimmy Dimicci, who queried, 'What'n hell's everyone gettin' het up about?'

But even Dimmy, who was not inaptly nicknamed, could sense the tension among the party of Legionnaires.

Partizans . . . the most dreaded of the inhabitants of the desert. Renegade Arabs mostly, with a few of other nationalities who had gone completely Arab in their way of life, they roamed the desert in the pay of France in search of *les poumpists* — deserters from the Foreign Legion.

They were essential to the maintenance

of France's desert army, for few men would have stayed long in the Legion if they had found it easy to escape. But France paid the *partizans* little as a standing force; they had to show results to earn their living.

For every deserter they caught in the act of fleeing, a bounty was paid to them. Only it wasn't paid if they brought in the deserter alive — only if the severed head could be produced.

The policy of savagery was deliberate. It kept men from thinking too readily of walking out into the desert in the hope of being befriended by some tribe of Arabs, as had happened at times. For the *partizans* went at will among the villages and routed out deserters and took their heads for the bounty they brought.

Sometimes, it was rumoured, the heads they brought in weren't deserters' at all, and that was why the Arabs in the caravan train were uneasy. Their heads, and some soldier's *matricule* (identity disc), would earn the reward, provided they had no hair on their face. The *partizans*, it was whispered among bearded Arabs, were good at shaving — heads.

Those men of evil rode slowly forward, covering the Legionnaires and Arabs alike. The officer looked down upon them from his beautiful, cream-coffee coloured stallion. He was a German, as all the desert knew, a man who had been a general, so it was rumoured, in the army of Rommel. Now he was a captain in the army of his vanquishers, content so long as he lived in this desert that had given him what his soul craved for.

He wasn't like a conventional, high-ranking Nazi officer. There was no monocle in his eye; instead, incongruous here in the desert, were neat, rimless eyeglasses. He looked more like an officer in a non-combatant unit, such as the Medical Corps, rather than a man with a fearsome record as a bloody warrior. Yet his very air of anaemic nervelessness somehow chilled these people before him.

For they knew that, bloody though his *partizans* were, this thin, sallow officer in Arab headdress outdid them all in ferocity. And one man there knew it better than any except the officer himself . . .

The be-glassed captain rode right up to the astonished sergeant, who gave a last-minute salute. The captain smiled, but it had all the humour of the open jaws of a python about to swallow its prey.

'Mon sergent,' he said, in the colourless, guttural French of the German, 'you do not deserve the honour invested in you in those two red chevrons you wear.'

The sergeant stood stiffly to attention, his eyes looking rigidly ahead. The officer was playing with the whip that some French Foreign Legion officers and sergeants carried. He stroked the lash through slim, sensitive fingers that had never known the need to work for a living.

'Your orders, as I well know, are to search all caravan trains thoroughly for the arms that may be carried in them. You, imbecile, have been put off by the threatening attitude of these, a race servile to the country you serve. You were afraid to risk their displeasure at carrying out your duty in searching the women's beasts. Mon petit, you will assuredly suffer for that lapse of duty.'

Before the eye could see, almost, that whiplash had curled round and bit across the face of the petrified sergeant. It hurt, but he was in too much terror even to show it, and he stood there and waited for the next blow.

Instead, that cold, dispassionate voice lashed him and reduced him to a shaking mass of terror.

'You will be reported when I reach your garrison. You will be given the hell that is with the zephyrs in their penal battalions, because softness must be found out and driven from the soul in hard expiation. I shall insist upon it because a weak sergeant is a danger to the men he leads and to all who serve with him. Scum, go thou to El Kwatra, there to await my return!'

A white-faced sergeant, who until that moment had been a bully and a brute to all weaker than himself, stumbled towards his horse. This was the end for him; that weakness in not conducting the search of the caravan to the bitter end had been his undoing. Never again would he show mercy, he was vowing, and then the thought died tremblingly on his lips.

Never again would he be able to show mercy or otherwise, for when this dreaded *partizan* captain made a threat it was known throughout the Legion that it was duly carried out. Captain Sturmer was a man with an influence far greater than the rank his uniform carried.

As he swung into his saddle, his comrades silent around him only the bubbling malevolence of the kneeling camels breaking the stillness that had followed the officer's threat, panic gripped him. He was to be disgraced. He would lose his rank He would be sent to the dreaded Penal Battalion at Algiers, there to work out his miserable life on the roads.

It was not to be contemplated in a man of spirit. Better by far death in this thirsty desert, he was thinking. But he hid his sudden leaping thoughts, saluted and duly turned in the direction of the distant fort.

When he had gone over the brow, so that only the deep trailing hoof marks in the sand showed that he had ever been here, the captain called to his men: 'There my children goes a man who has no thought of paying for his unsoldierly conduct. There rides a man intent on deserting.'

It was like casting red meat to starving desert wolves that word to his men. Eyes seemed to brighten, heads went back and bearded lips smacked with glee. In one second every horse's head was being pulled round burnouses flying. A gasp of relief went up from everyone's lips. Frank and Arab alike.

Then a word of command cracked like a whiplash from those bloodless lips and halted those *partizans* as surely as a master's voice holds back even ravening hounds.

'You and you will go,' ordered that officer with the prissy rimless glasses. 'You will follow him until he turns from the way that leads most directly to Fort El Kwatra, and when that happens . . . '

He didn't finish his sentence. Two *partizans* kicked their horses into a heavy, stumbling gallop up the shifting slope after the sergeant, and as they started everyone there knew that that sergeant was as good as dead already.

These *partizans* wouldn't bother about the way the man went. They would get his head and *matricule* and come back and say, 'It was as the *capitaine* prophesied. The man turned to flee, and then we were on to him. Truly our captain knows the hearts of men . . . '

When the men had gone, Captain Sturmer, who had done far worse things that this ranked as nothing in his mind, looked again at the Legionnaires and ordered, 'Continue the search of that train. *Vitement!*'

They jumped to it, eight frantic Legionnaires intent on averting the wrath that could so easily be directed upon them by this bloodthirsty man. And this time there wasn't so much as a murmur from those Arabs.

Tex leapt towards the camel that carried a blue-eyed Arab maiden. That was intriguing, though there were deeper thoughts on his mind since the arrival of the *partizans*. He bumped into Rube Koskowsci, who was known as 'The Schemer', and he saw that comrade's face sweating from more than exertion.

The Texan gave a tight grin and cracked. 'Why don't you figger up some scheme to get us outa here, wise guy?' Then he added, in disgust, 'An' you think you c'n get to Lake Cbad with Sturmer's *partizans* roamin' the desert!'

He looked up. The blue-eyed Arab maiden had drawn back the curtains and seemed to be listening. Tex took one look and said to 'The Schemer', 'Beat it. brother. This is my country.'

Some Arabs came running up then. They appeared terrified, as if torn between fear of the dreaded *partizans* and some other, unknown terror. Tex looked round and saw eyes on him that were horrified and incredulous, and he couldn't understand it. As if, he thought, there was something astonishing about his appearance.

He shrugged. His orders were unmistakable, and Sturmer and his vultures were sitting their horses in a position that enabled them to see that those orders were carried out. He had no alternative — unless he wished to suffer the fate of that sergeant in the desert.

His lips tightened. Now, more than ever before in his adventurous life, he wanted to live . . .

He reached up to help out the girl, and another shock came to him, one almost as great as that which had caused him to lose his grip on his rifle.

He saw those blue eyes again, above that silken *yashmak*. Saw the golden hair and wondered at it. And then a crisp voice came from under the square of silk, and it said, 'On your way, brother. Can't you see you're not wanted here?'

Tex stared incredulously, not believing his own ears. An American voice! An American girl, by the sound of it. It was staggering, stunning. When he realized that his senses hadn't tricked him, he thought, 'Holy gee, what's an American gal doin' in this neck o' the woods?'

He gulped, then caught a threatening movement from the impatient leader of the *partisans* and said briskly, 'Sorry, sister, but maybe you didn't understand the Legion French that that coyote back there uttered. He says, 'Get them gals outa their prams an' give 'em the once over'. Not you,' he added hastily, seeing the quick alarm come to her blue eyes. 'These damn' camels an' their loads.'

All around the womenfolk were protesting volubly, terrified out of their wits at the combination of hated Legionnaires and dreaded *partizans*, about whom no man, Arab or Frank, spoke good. They thought that abject, screaming terror might wring pity from their searchers, and accordingly the hot desert for miles around was filled with their wailing cries.

It moved Captain Sturmer to say that if it didn't stop he'd turn his whip loose among them.

Frantic Arab husbands and fathers shouted down their hysterical womenfolk. By the time this was done, under cover of the noise, several things had happened.

The American girl had tried to hold her position in the tent, watched uneasily, wretchedly, by the escorting Arabs. But big Legionnaire Texas had put one foot on the massive ribs of the kneeling camel and in one swift movement had the girl out in the sunshine. She struggled in his grip. And because he was off-balance he let her go and she fell into the soft sand. It didn't hurt her, but it affected her dignity, and Tex was tickled to hear some strong American words directed at himself.

He didn't wait. Sturmer was impatient and demanding swiftness to the search. Tex dragged aside the curtain and pulled himself half inside . . .

Someone was lying on one of the two soft mattresses that were slung on either side of the camel's hump. The girl would sit on one side, balancing her companion . . .

Tex saw a hand and a knife, and then realized that the travelling companion wasn't a woman.

It was a man, and he had a small black, pointed beard and it was the face of that young Arab that looked at him — the Arab he had captured and then helped to get away from the Legion.

4

Shock held Tex irresolute, hanging half in and half out of the silken tent on that angry, protesting camel's back. He saw the pallor of that young face and thought, 'He's wounded. Maybe he got hit, after all, escapin' the other night.'

Thoughts flashed through his mind. The young Arab must have stumbled on foot until he'd sighted this caravan. They had taken him to save his life, and perhaps they had put him with the American girl, reckoning the foreigner's nationality might save the camel from being searched and the wounded Arab from being discovered.

Only, he had been discovered, and ironically enough by the same Legionnaire who had been responsible not only for his capture but for his release!

Tex saw that hand lift, the knife about to come plunging at him. He saw the desperate, feverish eyes behind the blade.

And then, without thinking what he was doing, his head shook slightly.

The hand wavered. Tex let himself go and dropped down on to the yielding desert sand. When he turned he saw five brown-eyed Arabs and one blue-eyed American girl dressed in Arab maiden's clothes staring at him as if they had all taken leave of their senses.

And he was wondering if in fact he had taken leave of his senses. Why was he showing such mercy to this strange Arab? He was endangering his own neck in doing so, for if he were found out those hungry-looking *partizans* would have his head off in no time.

Yet deliberately he gave no sign that he had found anything amiss within that silken palanquin atop the camel. He wiped his face that was gritty where the blowing sand had stuck to the sweat. Through his fingers he saw those blue eyes, and they were changing from incredulity to the wildest of delight. It stirred Tex, made him feel that what he had done was worthwhile, to have won this girl's regard.

Not that he had done it for that reason, of course. Back of his mind had been the thought, 'If I pull this hombre out, them damn' vultures'll skewer him.' And he didn't want to see anybody skewered that afternoon. He soldiered for France, but that didn't make him vicious against her enemies.

'The fellar c'n have another chance,' was his thought. Anyway, judging by that deathly pallor and fever-bright eyes, the man was badly wounded. He mightn't have long to live, so let him die in peace, gradually and without brutal violence.

The American girl in those clinging silken robes that were so concealing and yet revealing, stepped forward. As she made to ascend her camel again, Tex caught the fervent whisper, 'Fellow, you're one great big man. If there's anything I can do for you . . . '

There was. Tex came out with it immediately, stooping to cup his hands so that she could swing inside the palanquin again.

'What's your phone number, babe?'

She saw the twinkle in his grey eyes

and told him. He shook his head. 'Ain't no good,' he murmured. It was a New York number.

He felt the warmth of her scented body as he lifted her. Then, just as she disappeared in alongside the wounded Arab, he felt her hand pat him lightly on the shoulder. It seemed to leave him tingling. Now he had no doubts that he had done the right thing in shielding the Arab . . . for undoubtedly he had won approval in those eyes, and they were mighty lovely eyes, he was thinking.

He went on to search the next camel. Within minutes they were through. They had a corporal with them, a slovenly man who owed his position to his propensity for telling what men had in their minds and so securing them punishment for sins contemplated and not actually performed. Now he was terrified — so much so, he could hardly stand.

He remembered what had happened to the sergeant, and now he was in charge of the party and had to go forward and make his report. His legs wouldn't take him.

Elegant shoved him in the back and propelled him forward a couple of strides. They were delighted to see the N.C.O.'s discomfiture; hadn't he made them all suffer in some way in his time?

Elegant's best Brooklyn yapped, 'So what, the guy c'n only chop off your head!'

'The Camel' helped him another couple of paces, then opened his long yellow teeth in that long, squashed face and grunted, 'It ain't no head to be proud of, so whatja got to lose?'

Then the 'Scourge of the Desert' began to turn in his saddle, becoming impatient. The corporal leapt forward like the wind, prepared to risk anything rather than earn this thin captain's displeasure.

He saluted wildly, stammered, *Mon Capitaine*, we have made a search and found nothing.'

'You are fools, then,' said Captain Sturmer without heat. 'For assuredly if the spirit is willing, always fault can be found with these dogs of Arabs.'

But he let it pass. Two *partizans* were galloping down the rolling dune towards them, their horses sinking to their knees because of a combination of weight and slope. They hadn't been away long. Every eye except the corporal's and the man who addressed him were turned on those two evil creatures.

The captain gave orders. 'You will report that your sergeant was detected by me, Captain Herman Sturmer, to be neglecting his duty. You will tell your commanding officer that he was ordered to return and report himself for this misdemeanour, but he chose to attempt to desert.'

The captain hadn't looked round as his two horsemen rode up. All eyes now were on a bundle that one rider carried before him. Something round was wrapped in a dirty cloth. The captain gave a jerk with his left hand and immediately the *partizans* came forward, stooped from his saddle, and deposited the bundle into the hands of the horrified corporal. Something warm wetted his fingers.

Those rimless glasses that gave the captain an unseeing look surveyed the quaking man dispassionately. 'You will take back evidence that *les partizans* were alert and alive to their duty,' his thin, colourless voice intoned. 'We will call upon your officer within a few days to collect what is due to us for detecting this *poumpist* . . . '

Something curious happened then. As if for the first time, Captain Sturmer saw the tall Legionnaire from Texas, His voice trailed away, as if puzzled. Then he started to speak again, but his eyes were upon Tex. Up on her camel a girl with blue eyes was noticing it. She kept lifting her camera, then feverishly turning the reel to another frame for yet another picture. For this was why she had come all this way and under such hardships. Her soul was thrilling. She had done it, after all. Soon she would be on her way to the coast, and then . . .

Captain Sturmer's thin, imperious voice came clearly over the silent desert air. 'This caravan will not go through to the coast. It will travel, my corporal, under your escort to Fort El Kwatra, and there it will remain until I finish my patrol and am able to meet your commanding officer.'

Texas's head started to turn in shock at the news. The fort was no place for that wounded Arab, or for that blue-eyed girl posing as an Arab. Then, in time, he stopped the involuntary movement. Sturmer's glasses were still turned full on him.

Back of him he heard sharp exclamations of dismay and concern from the Arabs, many of whom understood Legion French as well as he did. He heard interpretations, and then the murmur of irate Arab voices began to rise high on the desert air. They didn't want to go near that dreaded fort. They were even saying they would not go there.

And then Captain Sturmer lifted one imperious hand; the hungry-looking *partizans* shifted in their saddles, and Lebels were pointing again at the Arabs, and unsheathed, sharp edged Arab swords — *flissas* — were in their right hands.

No Arab spoke of disobeying after that. Tex was thinking, 'Why? Why? Why make this caravan go an' stop in that stinkin' hole for a few days?' What advantage was it to Sturmer — or to the Legion?'

Then he realized that Sturmer was speaking again, looking now at the corporal. Sturmer had dropped his voice, and his manner had changed. He had the appearance of a man who is faced with big problems, from which could emerge grave danger.

Tex wasn't supposed to overhear, but he was near and caught something of what was being said.

'Tell . . . commander . . . Arabs grouping in the southern mountains. Messengers are travelling the length and breadth of the country . . . holy war, perhaps . . . whispered that soon the Arabs will have all the arms and ammunition they want . . . '

And then Captain Sturmer spoke a name.

'Sheik Abdul el Nuhas is returning from exile to lead them.'

Abdul el Nuhas, the Arab fighter who had so bravely led his people against the tyrannical French in the wars of three years ago. He had been exiled and was now reported to be living in honour in Egypt.

So Nuhas was coming back, thought Tex. That meant big trouble — it might even become a holy war, as Sturmer opined.

Then Sturmer was speaking again, and again only the corporal was supposed to hear what he said, but in the Legion a man grew long ears.

'Tell commander . . . detain caravan . . . use people as hostages. Rumour . . . El Kwatra is first post to be attacked.'

Tex understood the captain's tactics now. This man certainly was an efficient officer. Now he would be riding across the trails that led from Libya, watching for the returning sheik to enter into French territory. He and his *partizans* were the eyes of the French desert intelligence system, and good eyes, too.

The corporal saluted and stumbled away, glad to be still alive. He began to shout and curse, because cursing should always accompany shouting in the Legion, and in very terror of those sinister *partizans* who were impartial in their head-cutting exploits, the camel leaders kicked their grunting beasts on to their feet and turned along the trail left by the sergeant who was now dead.

The captain sat his horse in silence, those rimless glasses reflecting the desert glare so that no one saw his eyes. But Tex knew they never left him. He strode across to his horse and swung into the saddle lithely, like the born horseman he was. Looking straight before him, he rode alongside the protesting column of camels, swaying and weaving their long necks as they padded on great flat feet through the shifting sand.

When he was alongside the officer, a sharp order rang out, 'You, Legionnaire. *Venez!*'

Tex turned his horse, his face immobile, but he had to hold himself in as he gave the customary salute.

Legionnaire faced officer. Those glasses on that thin face under the Arab head-dress concealed what the eyes were thinking. Sturmer said, unemotionally, 'I seem to have seen you before. Where?' Short, brutal, straight to the point.

Tex shrugged. '*Mon capitaine*, I do not remember the honour. In my life I have never seen you before a half-hour ago.' And he was speaking the truth.

Sturmer wasn't so sure. 'Your name?' he rapped

'Legionnaire Texas.'

'Texas?' Sturmer's head lifted at that. 'Texas is the name of a country, not a man,' he said ironically, but he didn't persist with his questioning. Many men took fanciful names when they joined the Legion, in preference to using their own. It did not do for an officer to enquire too closely into the reasons for the change.

Sturmer nodded, dismissing the Legionnaire. In the same instant he pulled round his beautiful, coffee-cream stallion and sent it loping away towards the south. The fierce, hungry-looking *partizans*, like hounds deliberately kept on short diet to make them savage, swept in behind him, riding in his dust. Within moments they were out of sight.

The caravan creaked and rocked its way toward the fortress, every man and woman occupied by his or her thoughts. None of them was pleasant.

The girl with blue eyes was thinking, 'Well, for cryin' out loud!' And looking at her camera she wondered what the penalty was for taking pictures in a military area.

Big, rangy Legionnaire Texas, riding alongside her camel watched until Sturmer had disappeared. He was thinking, 'I met him. It's him, all right.' There was satisfaction in his mind, and yet he was filled with the anger that follows frustration. For though they had met, he had been unable to reveal his identity, as he had wanted. Those *partizans* weren't to be trifled with.

'Another time,' he sighed. A last look at the lifting dust cloud that alone showed the passage of those hunters of men in this arid desert. Those savage man-hunters who followed a man more ferocious than the lot put together, for all his prissy eyeglasses . . .

That man who had brutally killed a thousand prisoners, and all American, within a few miles only of where they were riding now . . .

Dimmy came riding up to Texas. His heavy, dough-like face showed cunning. He said, confidentially, 'I got that fellar cut out for size, Tex. You know what?' Tex shook his head. 'I figger he ain't a good guy. I gotta hunch he's mean an' bad.' And he nodded his big turnip head to add significance to his words,

Tex said, admiringly, 'Now, that's mighty smart o' you, Dimmy. We wouldn't have known it. You go an' tell the corp what you just figgered out, in case he ain't tumbled to it.'

Dimmy beamed and threw out his chest and felt goldarned smart, and then spurred on to give his news to the corporal. From the other side of that lurching camel, which looked evil; and smelled worse, Tex heard Elegant on the eternal business of sassing Louie the Camel,

Elegant was yapping brightly, 'You know what, Louie, I was talkin' to you back there for ten minutes an' you never said a word to me.'

Silence. Then Louie's ill-tempered voice, suspicious because Elegant was always trying to take a rise out of him, 'I never was back there, Brooklyn. I bin here all the time, I reckon.'

'Sure,' came that bright, yapping voice.

Tex could almost see the smile of happiness on that flat, good-natured pan of Elegant's. 'It wuz only when I saw it didn't have no cigarette in its mouth that I realised my mistake. So help me, Louie, I'd bin talkin' to a camel, a real camel!'

Louie bit. Up came that savage temper. 'By jeepers,' he snarled. 'Some day I'm gonna take you apart an' I'll do it a way that hurts you more'n terrible. Wise guy!'

Tex thought he'd go round and pick up the bits. The two Legionnaires were alongside each other, Elegant with a look of blissful delight on his face, Louie seeming ready to bite him. Louie, with his squashed head and craggy nose and teeth that were long and yellow, like a camel's.

Elegant said, soothingly, 'Okay, brudder. I ain't scared. I ain't scared o' nuttin' that comes from the Bronx.'

Louie snarled. 'What'n the hell's Brooklyn got to be proud of? Just a bridge.'

'An' wharrer bridge. You ain't got no bridge like it.'

'We gotta zoo,' snapped Louie.

And that was a tactical error. Elegant

jumped in with a quick 'Yeah, an' some o' their camels got out an' joined the Foreign Legion.'

Tex reached forward and grabbed the hand that was going to flatten Elegant's battered features even further. He said chidingly, 'Why don't you two mavericks lay off? Stop yellin' an' keep an eye on these Ay-rabs. You never know with Ay-rabs what's gonna happen next.' And again he sighed for those revolvers he had once worn. Colts were the thing for close-quarters work, not clumsy, slow-shooting Lebels.

Louie jerked his horse's mouth and rode ahead of them. Tex watched him go, rolling himself a cigarette in a way that fascinated the Legion — one-handed, and using only three fingers at that.

'You wanna lay off, brother,' he warned. 'Louie's more like a camel than you think. One day he's gonna bite you, an' they say a camel bite's pretty fatal.'

Elegant pooh-poohed the idea. 'Aw, you don't know Louie. He ain't bad. It's just the guy comes from the Bronx, an' it makes him sensitive. You ever bin to the

Bronx?' His small, good-tempered eyes regarded the cowboy from Texas quizzically. 'Nope. I reckon you ain't. It's a dump, fellar. One helluva dump. Gives a fellar a kind of inferiority complex.' He was proud of those two words; he'd learned them recently and had been busting to use them. He went on, 'Now Brooklyn, that's the place to live in. Brooklyn's sure got everything.'

'If it's got everything,' asked an American voice, 'why did you leave it, soldier?'

It was the girl, leaning from her palanquin. She was still wearing that silk across the bridge of her nose, and Tex had an impulse to reach up and remove it. He wanted to know what sort of a face went with those lovely blue eyes. He thought, 'She'll have nice, apple-blossom skin, soft, rounded cheeks and lips . . . '

He stopped thinking of her lips. In the Legion men saw little of women and it affected him to think of this hidden beauty. True, in the *village negres* or in the cafés around Sidi-bel-Illah there were dancing girls and entertainers and women who would drink with a man provided he had money. But they were coarsened by their mode of life, and had little in the way of feminine attraction. All right for Dimmy, Tex thought, but for him — blue eyes and fair hair and an American voice to match his own!

Elegant shifted uneasily in his saddle at the question. Then he said, frankly, 'Me, I saw a film. It wuz in Technicolor, and the dames . . . ' His voice went up in ecstasy.

'A Foreign Legion film — and it brought you all this way to the desert!' She sounded amused.

Big legionnaire Texas reached across and tried to pull the curtains wider. She resisted, yet she knew he was aware of what was in that palanquin beside her. So he said, meekly, 'What brought you here, sister?'

She didn't tell him. Dimmy was riding back, looking pleased. The girl hadn't taken her eyes off the big, rangy Texan in that uniform of blue tunic, white pants and *kepi* with neck curtains. A glamorous man, she was thinking; as handsome in his hard-bitten way as any hero of a Foreign Legion film.

Softly she asked, clinging to that swaying contraption, 'What's your name, brother?'

He said, 'Hank,' his eyes on Dimmy. Dimmy was looking pleased and carrying something. Mechanically, hardly thinking of what he was saying, the Legionnaire went on, 'But most guys call me Tex, on account I've got the surname. Texas . . . '

His voice trailed away. Dimmy had wheeled his horse alongside them. On his saddlebow rested a bloody bundle. That big, moon-face that was like a bladder of lard only about two-thirds as intelligent creased into a happy smile.

'That corporal thinks I'm smart,' he said proudly, 'When I told him what I thought of that guy with the glasses, you know what he said? 'Mong dew, is it possible?' Then he shoved this on to me. Said I was a smart fellar, an could hold the meat ration till we reached the fort.'

His pride changed to puzzlement. The girl had withdrawn with a strangled cry, unable to look at that thing in Dimmy's hands. Elegant and Louie simultaneously spurred away up the swaying line of soft-treading beasts.

Tex was kinder. He said. 'Brother, if you don't beat it down wind from me pronto, there'll be another dead head aroun' the place.'

Dimmy didn't get it, but rode away. This was one heck of a world, he thought, grieved, when a fellar didn't get any credit for being smart.

Two hours later a sullen train of Arabs filed through the big gate of the post at El Kwatra. An astonished garrison watched their arrival, and then a whisper went up as the womenfolk were seen within their palanquins, and hungry-eyed men began to press nearer. Tex thought, 'There's goin' to be trouble. Keepin' women here, among this pack o'wolves, will sure make life interestin'.'

The parade ground was packed with camels, Legionnaires and Arabs. The legion officers and N.C.O.S bellowed contradictory orders at the unhappy Arabs, who shrieked and behaved viciously towards their camels, and they in turn filled the air with the hideous noise of their snarling, bubbling voices.

In time, when the corporal had made his report, order was restored. The Arabs were allowed to pitch their tents against one wall of the fort, and then the camels were led outside to be picketed and watched by a Legionnaire guard. That gave a bit more room within the post, as well as removing the odour of sweating camels.

Dimmy handed over his trophy to a commander who wrinkled his face distastefully but went through the routine of checking known features against the *matricule* that accompanied the head. Then he ordered it to be burned, and ordered that Dimmy should not be allowed anywhere near him until he had been thoroughly bathed in the *lavabo*.

Dimmy couldn't understand it. There wasn't a man who had stayed near him since his arrival at the post.

Tex went into his barrack room and sank down gratefully on his bed. He had much to think of, and he was weary from his day in the saddle. Next day he would be even wearier, he knew, because he would have to go through his pack drill under the instruction of a sergeant made more than usually brutal because of the interruption to his siesta.

The Schemer came to his side. He came so quickly, and sat down and looked all around in such a series of jerky motions, that Tex knew immediately he was on to something.

High up on the ramparts outside a sentry called out a few excited words to his guard corporal.

Tex drawled, 'You're gonna tell me you've just thought up another scheme. Right?'

'Right. Don't you see, big fellar, all this has played into our hands?' Tex looked at those bright blue eyes, and the shining, red-cheeked face, and wished he could find enthusiams to sustain him as Rube Koskowsci did.

'What's played into our hands?'

The guard corporal was shouting to the sergeant of the guard. Some of the men were moving towards the open door.

'Why, these camels parked right out-side,' whispered the Schemer. 'We'll need camels. Some night when we're supposed to be on guard we'll just ride off south on them blamed hump wagons.'

Tex said, 'Yeah?' without interest. It got Rube mad.

'What're you lyin' there for, yeahin' me?' he demanded. 'Ain't it a good scheme? Ain't it the best yet? Don't we all want to get outa this hell hole, an' ain't that the best way outa it?' He was indignant. He never could understand why people didn't share his enthusiasm for his bright ideas.

Tex said, 'It's a good scheme. Maybe I'll take you up on it soon. Just now I'm tired. Let's all get some rest, includin' them camels, then we'll talk about goin' on pump.'

But Tex didn't give the real reason why he wouldn't think of leaving the post right then. He found he couldn't go and leave a blue-eyed American girl cooped up with these wolves of Legionnaires. Besides, there was a job for him to do, the reason why he had joined this crazy Foreign Legion that seemed deliberately to drive men mad. And going on pump didn't seem the way to achieve his ends . . . Or was it? Hadn't things changed . . . ?

He put The Schemer off, though maybe later he might be glad of an opportunity to break out from El Kwatra. but not now, not just at this moment.

Outside there was a sudden babel of sound, as of many voices raised, and then a curious silence that seemed to hang over the post. It wasn't natural, that silence, and those men still remaining within the whitewashed walls of their quarters sat up and wondered and then began to hurry out to find out the cause of it.

Tex went with them, as much as anything to end the talk with the red-cheeked Rube. Rube was still arguing, making a last-minute effort to change Tex's mind and throw in with the scheme, but it seemed that Tex wasn't listening.

Every man was up on the catwalks, looking out over the desert. Tex started instinctively to reach for a Lebel, and then realized that not only were the men up on the ramparts without weapons, but the gate was lifted to receive whoever might come in. Clearly this was no enemy that had attracted the Legionnaires' attention, but if not, what was it?

Tex strode across to the open gate that could be dropped into position in a matter of seconds — like a guillotine and as effective if a man got his head in the way. The captain and his lieutenants were already there, attracted by the shouts of the men. The *Chef* was doubling up, fastening his tight tunic, and a couple of sergeants were coming across from siesta.

And then silence reigned, not a man watching making a sound.

Tex and his fellow American looked through the open gateway. They saw a lone figure toiling towards them across the soft, blistering hot sand. That figure wore a tunic that was blue, Tex noted, and his interest was instantly alerted as much as those other watchers up on the ramparts.

The man came nearer. No one went out to greet him. Everyone was too amazed for that.

They could only stand and gape.

For this was the dead man come back to life.

When he halted, fifty yards from the gateway, and lifted up a black-stubbled face, those sharp eyes recognized it at once.

It was Ca-ca.

5

At that there was a rush, and men went out to support him and help the weary, dirty Legionnaire through the gate.

The little captain grew emotional. As Ca-ca was borne towards him he saluted him on both cheeks, crying, 'Here is a soldier! We left him for dead, and now he returns to us. It is remarkable, it is marvellous. It is something beyond comprehension that he should return.' And then he tired of drama, and said, practically, 'What happened to you, dog? Quick! Out with your story, for this accursed sun is hot and I want to return to my quarters.'

Ca-ca lifted eyes that were bleary from the dust that had blown into them. His voice was feeble, as if the strength had left him.

'*Mon capitaine*,' he said in that exhausted voice, 'when I was bitten by that accursed sand viper, I ran for very madness and perhaps it saved my life. Indeed I have heard that violent exercise does sometimes pump the poison out of one's system.'

'Quick, quick,' demanded the little captain. 'We are not here to enquire into your system. What happened then?'

'I fell,' declared Ca-ca. He looked round. 'Did not everyone see me fall?' Tex was watching him, never missing an inflection of the voice, nor a gesture of the hand or movement of that dirty, sweat-grimed face.

'My senses must have left me then,' Ca-ca declared, and smote his head to show how empty it had been at the time. 'It was night and dark and all was quiet when I came to once more. I was wracked in agony. I was sick as no man has ever been sick before.' And he made expressive pantomime of vomiting until the captain irritably declared that it made him sick to watch him.

'So then you came back?'

'All day I lay and was ill, then with night I set off for the fort, but must have grown delirious and wandered. Today I thought I would go mad until I came across tracks leading to the post. '*Mon Dieu*,' he ended pathetically, 'I am glad to back with my gallant comrades.'

Everyone was touched, forgetting in the emotion of that moment that Ca-ca, a true Apache of the Paris gutter, was a man not to be trusted, a man who had done things to his comrades more times than one. The captain said again that he was a good soldier, to return of his own free will to the Legion, and not try to escape like some dogs did. He would be excused duties for the next twenty-four hours, he ended magnanimously, and then strode off to ogle the Arab maidens on his way to his quarters.

When the enthusiastic crowd of Legionnaires had departed with Ca-ca, the hero of the hour, Tex also strolled across to where the tents had been erected against the fortress wall.

He found a few other men loitering there, attracted by the knowledge that there were women within those tents, and hopefully waiting for the miracle of a favour from them. There wasn't anything better to do within the fort, anyway.

Legionnaire Texas heard his name whispered as he went by. 'Hi, Tex!' The girl's voice. He hesitated, looked round and then sat against the wall next to the tent. The girl spoke through to him.

'How long will they keep us here, big fellar?'

Tex looked round. No one seemed to be watching, but he replied with his lips as still as he could keep them.

'I don't know. All I know is, these wolves'll sure make trouble with you gals aroun' the joint.'

There was silence, then the American girl said, 'I'm not so bothered about that. Tex. What worries me is — him.'

'The Ay-rab?'

'The Ay-rab,' she mimicked. Then the humour departed from her voice, and in its place was a little frantic note. 'Tex, can't you do something? He's feverish from his wounds, and at times he raves and if he isn't careful, so help me, the whole fort will know we have a wounded Arab with us!'

Tex sighed. He seemed to have let

himself in for a lot in not disclosing the presence of that wounded man. He said, 'Sister, he's all yours. There ain't a thing I c'n do to help you, I reckon.'

Through the tent wall he heard her say, softly, 'But you would, if you could, wouldn't you, Tex?'

He said, 'For your blue eyes, babe, I'd do anythin'. Just call me Hank an' see the difference it makes.'

So she said, 'Hank, you've got to help us escape. I won't see a suffering man turned over to these brutes of Foreign Legion officers.' There was a catch in her voice. She was thinking of that sergeant that afternoon, and the captain on the lovely, cream-and-coffee coloured stallion. 'I — I've seen enough brutality for one day.'

Texas sighed. 'I don't see how it can be done,' he was saying, and then his mind went to Rube Koskowsci and the scheme he had put up. Bluntly he said, 'To help you would mean goin' on pump, an' you've seen what happens to *poumpists* today, haven't you?'

He had to explain what he meant by

going on pump. The girl hadn't been in contact much with the Legion, evidently.

He growled, 'Mebbe I'll get someone to help you though, sister.' It made him bad tempered at the thought. If anyone helped this girl, he wanted to be that man. She had courage — guts, he would have said.

'But won't you come?' His heart beat a little faster the quick way she spoke.

'Nope . . . I've got business to do.'

She was quick. She came back immediately with — 'Business . . . with that captain of the *partizans*?'

He didn't deny it, didn't admit it.

She said, 'Then he'll lose his head. Tex! I saw the way you first looked at him, when you dropped your rifle. Tex, why do you hate that man so? I heard you say you had never met him before in your life.'

Tex rose to his feet, his shadow throwing long before him. 'It was true, what I said.' And then it was his turn to ask questions. 'Who are you? What's your name? What're you doin' with this Ay-rab outfit?'

She said, 'Call me Souriya — '

'That's Arabic.'

'And I'm an Arab girl for the duration of this trip. That's all I'm telling you now, brother.'

Tex walked away grumbling, 'That's a fine thing to say to a fellar who's got to persuade his comrade to go on pump with you.'

He stopped. He had bumped into a man. He looked up and saw it was La Femme.

La Femme smiled a smile that was maidenly sweet. His long, dark lashes dropped modestly over eyes that any girl would have given a lot to possess. Tex caught the soft, murmured voice, 'It is the *cafard* that makes a man speak aloud to himself, the beetle that crawls in one's brain.'

Tex agreed. 'It is the *cafard*,' he said, and moved to go past. He was two paces beyond when he heard that soft, musical voice again.

La Femme said, 'Unless one has been fortunate and made an assignment with some girl inside one of those tents . . . '

His voice trailed away. It was deliberate. That was La Femme — to hint and not say outright, as a woman would. And yet his meaning was quite clear.

The Legionnaire from Texas brought his head round. His eyes were so narrowed that not a glimmer showed of grey pupils within. La Femme saw a face as hard as the desert rock, a lean, strong face — the face of a fighting man who wasn't to be crossed, and suddenly regretted his temerity of a moment before.

Tex's voice spoke words that almost tinkled with ice. 'One day, hombre, somethin' bad's gonna happen to that pretty face of yourn. Watch your tongue or it might happen now.'

Then he turned on his heel and left the man. La Femme gulped, and his hand involuntarily rose to his soft cheek that had never known a razor. He was as proud of his beauty as any girl, and the thought of disfigurement horrified him and shook him to the depths.

Even so — perhaps out of malice — that evening it was whispered throughout the barrack rooms that there were girls within those tents who would talk with Legionnaires. It made men lie on their beds and stare at whitewashed ceilings and think.

Tex's thoughts were on other things. Sturmer's presence in the vicinity made a lot of difference. After a while he came to a decision. When he was sure of his own mind, he rose and went across to where The Schemer, face beaming with pleasure, was engaged on *astiquage* — that polishing and cleaning of one's equipment that never ceased in the Legion. Curiously, some men seemed to delight in the fatigue, but not careless, casual hombres like big Tex.

He dropped on to the bed beside his comrade, drawled, 'How long d'you need, brother?'

Rube's industrious hand stopped. His head came round with the swiftness of a puppet's. His eyes were questioning, not daring to believe the thought that had jumped into his mind upon Tex's words. Cautiously he asked, 'For what, Tex?'

Tex merely jerked his head. He didn't need to say more.

Rube dropped his belt and polishing rag and drew in a breath so deep it seemed he would never stop inhaling. Then he let it out in a sigh that was equally long, a sigh redolent of relief.

He said, 'Say, a coupla days. Time to win some grub from the cookhouse, an' have plenty of water stashed out where them camels are.' Rube's mind was clicking over. Action was a stimulant to the man, and now his fertile mind was plotting, examining details and rejecting or accepting them.

'Yeah, that means fixing for some of us to get on the camel guard. We c'n take a lot out in twenty-four hours.' He went on enthusiastically to give further details, but Tex interrupted him.

'I've changed my mind, brother. I'm comin' with you but only on one condition.'

'Say it. We'll need you, Tex,' Rube answered.

'Two others must come along, too. A wounded Ay-rab and — a girl.'

Rube said, 'A girl!' and whistled. Then he stopped whistling, because men were looking curiously at this Legionnaire who could find something to be excited about.

Rube recommenced his polishing. Out

102

of the corner of his mouth he demanded, 'Can you fix for them to get out to the camels?'

Tex rose. 'I'll try,' he said. 'Okay, then, Rube. We make the break two nights from now, huh?'

'Two nights from now,' said Rube softly, his eyes shining. In forty-eight hours from now they would be quitting this accursed Foreign Legion, would be heading in a direction that would be least expected — due south, right across the Sahara, right across the continent of Africa itself. It would be hazardous, but Rube thought their chances of survival would be at least as great as if remaining in the dreaded Legion.

Tex went across to his bed. He felt sick. He hadn't told Rube why he was suddenly encouraging desertion.

They were to act as decoys, to bring an enemy after them. That enemy might be too strong, in which event the *poumpists* — and the Arab and maybe the girl — would go under. Tex thought, 'If we do, maybe it would be better for the gal if she loses her head, too.'

The *partizans* wouldn't be nice to — what was her name? Souriya. He drowsed. It was a nice name, but phoney, of course. As phoney as Texas . . . Probably she was Ellen Smith or Esther Van Reinfeld, or some name like that. But not Souriya . . . Not with those blue eyes . . .

★ ★ ★

Screams of fury woke the barrack room at dawn. It was Ca-Ca, having a tantrum. Dimmy, coming in from a night's guard duty, had tripped and spilt hot *jus* — that morning pot of bad coffee — all over the sleeping Legionnaire. The coffee might be bad, but it was also very hot.

In a moment there was uproar. Men, bad-tempered from having been brought from dreams back to this hellhole in the desert, shouted and took sides. Poor Dimmy was bewildered and could just stand, his pudding face turning from one speaker to another.

It encouraged Ca-Ca, who had all the instincts of a bully, though usually he did mean things in a more stealthy way. Talking volubly, his brown eyes big and molten and full of outraged wrath, suddenly he reached out, took the enamel pot out of Dimmy's unsuspecting hand, and then pitched the hot coffee grounds straight into those vacant eyes.

And then Ca-Ca, who was vile at heart, kicked the blinded Legionnaire and doubled him in agony on the floor.

A roar went up at that, mostly of approval. For men suffered so much themselves in this accursed Legion that it made them feel better if they saw someone else in torment for a change.

It encouraged Ca-Ca, who hadn't got over being a hero yesterday. His foot drew back and then he remembered he was without boots, so he picked up his belt and swung it viciously.

That belt never met its mark. A hand like steel grabbed the uplifted wrist. It gripped, and the fingers suddenly lost strength and the belt clattered to the floor. Ca-Ca, in pain, turned on his toes, for that giant strength had lifted him off his heels.

He looked into the hard, brown face of Texas.

Tex threw him crashing against the wall. Ca-Ca, in fury at being manhandled, came hurtling back. Eager Legionnaires immediately formed a ring and bellowed encouragement that was fated to bring attention upon them within minutes.

Ca-Ca did not favour *le box*. For him it was *savate* — the fight with feet even though unfortunately his were unshod at that moment. But even unshod feet can hurt more than fists, and most Legionnaires had feet so toughened by constant marching that they were as insensitive to pain as lumps of wood — and as hard.

His foot lashed up to kick the American where he would be crippled immediately. The Texan swayed back slightly, contempt on his lean, hard face. God a'mighty, didn't he know all these roughhouse tricks? Hadn't he fought in mining ramps, with timber men, railroad toughies, in saloons along the Mexican border and at rodeos and out on the range? Kicking . . .

He treated the Apache with contempt. His hands shot out and gripped that kicking leg on the ankle and under the knee. He crouched, exerting his full strength as he did so. That leverage on the extended leg was too great for the weight of the man. Miraculously, it seemed, Ca-Ca's body rose in the air and again hit the whitewashed wall with a thud. If he had hit with his head he would have been out, but his shoulder took the force of the blow and he came reeling back, his face murderous, intent on savaging this tall, lean American.

It was a curious fight, inside that yelling mob of naked and nearly naked men, just out from their beds. Both contestants were barefooted and bare above the midriff. Tex was wearing white fatigue pants, hastily donned, while Ca-Ca only wore the trunks that he slept in, those hot nights.

Ca-Ca kept rushing, kicking and hacking, and hitting with anything he could lay his hands on. For a few seconds, before the fury of the onslaught, the big Texan gave ground. He wasn't concerned, however. He let the Frenchman waste his strength, and then, when Ca-Ca's breath was gone, he stepped in, both hands swinging, his shoulders moving rhythmically.

Left-right, left-right. The crowd howled as Ca-Ca's head snapped back before the tearing blows of those hammer fists. Left-right again, and a glazed look came to those brown, Apache eyes. Ca-Ca tried to fight back, but the vigour was suddenly gone. Those mighty blows had the strength out of him.

Then his back was to the wall, and he could retreat no further. Ca-Ca was no craven. He stood there, ready to take his punishment, as was to be expected in the Legion. His long, sallow face was bloody, his eyes puffed up from contact with those fists. His hands lifted to ward off the blows, while the crowd shrieked, as crowds always do, for the kill.

But Tex brushed aside that guard, and instead of hitting the man he caught him by the neck and pinned him against the wall.

'Ca-Ca,' he growled, 'I don't like guys that hit my friends. I don't like guys that do dirty, kickin' tricks, anyway. An' if ever I see you do a thing like you did to Dimmy, I'll tear your guts out — see?'

Ca-Ca saw. He said nothing, but stood panting there, murder in his heart and evil in his closing eyes. He could not understand why he wasn't being beaten to a jelly, why this lean Texan talked instead of acted. But he was glad of it, though not grateful.

Tex's hand dropped away. Immediately, though, it fastened on the arm that had been nursed while the man had screamed that a viper had bitten it while he rested.

Ca-Ca saw the grey eyes searching it, twisting it to look behind, and in sudden panic he tried to pull it away. But that grip was too strong.

Tex said cynically, 'That warn't no viper bit you, brother.' He let the arm drop, but stood facing the swaying, beaten Legionnaire. Softly his voice went on. 'An' you weren't restin', either. You an' your buddies were standin' aroun' a tin when it happened.'

He stopped. Uncannily, silence had fallen in that barrack room. Men were listening, wondering, and the air seemed filled with drama. Tex realized that men were coming quickly through towards him.

Out of the corner of his eye he saw faces — faces taut with fear and desperation.

The Weeper's, whose left eye ran continuously.

Mervin Petrie who had sliced off men's heads and was in the Legion to save his own.

The Bulgar, big and brutal, with a soul as rotten as the teeth in his ugly, snarling head.

Jacques Quelclos was suddenly there. too; that little man who hated the world because he had been born small and was overlooked when he wasn't the butt of men's jokes and humour — Dwarf Quelclos who had no sense of humour and felt it intolerable that he should be overlooked, anyway.

La Femme was there, too, and he was the most evil of them all, for he preyed upon the weakest, and his methods were sly. He was a man utterly corrupted by every vice that was to be learned in the cities of the world, and the evil of it all was that his face gave no sign of the mind within.

Tex looked round, straight into their

eyes, meeting them one after another in turn. Instantly he was, mentally speaking, on his toes. For why should men show such tremendous concern at the words he was saying? He tried to think back, tried to remember everything concerning that moment in the desert just a few seconds before the Arab attack.

Then his eyes went back to Ca-Ca, and it seemed to him that that man's face was horrified.

Deliberately he probed, baiting them, trying to understand. For he had a feeling that here was something tremendously deep, something of importance that was to affect all their lives. These faces said so — these men weren't to be moved by little things. Their concern and . . . was it panic, he began to wonder . . . suggested the fear of death!

'I saw you, way back. You were lookin' fer somethin'. Could be it was a sand viper, huh?' he shot at them. Their faces froze, and he knew he was on the right track. 'You found one — stuck it in a tin that Cheauvin emptied.' His eyes flickered to Ca-Ca, watching tautly, as if dreading to hear more.

'You shoved me under the captain's hoss because I let on I knew what was in that tin, hombre. I hadn't forgotten that, fellar, an' I was just waitin' my time to take you to pieces for it.'

He went back to that tin. 'Eight hours later you used that viper, didn't you? You dropped it out of the tin an' ran away screamin' you'd been bitten.'

'You saw it — it did bite!' — Ca-Ca, quickly.

'We all saw it,' said Cheauvin, The Weeper, quickly.

'Did you not see me stamp on the thing?' queried Mervin Petrie, his pock-marked face intense as he shoved it threateningly forward.

'Was not our comrade foaming at the mouth?' That was little Quelclos, becoming truculent, as he always did.

Tex said gently, 'Soap. A little pellet in the mouth, and, *voila*, a man can froth as much as he likes!'

There was dead silence in the barrack room. Now the men there realized that the principals in this drama, which had such depth and yet was unknown to them were this lean Texan and the six men of whom Ca-Ca was the leader . . . Ca-Ca who was whispered to be a renegade against his own country.

The group stood close around Tex, their manner threatening. But he talked back at them, softly, completely sure that he could handle this situation just as he had handled Ca-Ca minutes before.

'Yeah . . . ' The story was beginning to clear in his own mind. 'There was no bite. Ca-Ca wanted a vacation before he got taken inside El Kwatra. That snake was dropped so as to provide the excuse — the froth on his lips was so much trimming to bear out the story.'

He remembered the startled look on the 'stricken' man's face as, in the act of plunging away towards the purple shadows, the Arab attack had begun. That wasn't according to plan, he thought. But by that time there was no turning back for Ca-Ca. Then he had to go through with his act of being a dying man, running crazily away into the gathering darkness.

Tex looked round at those men and saw the fear in their eyes. He asked gently, 'Why should a man wish to spend a vacation in the desert?'

But no one would explain the mystery. No one spoke and said why Ca-Ca should be satisfied and return to his unit at the end of a couple of days.

Texas shrugged. He spoke as calmly as ever. 'I know the desert. We have deserts as great as these in my country, and we have snakes that burrow into the sand. Let me tell you, though, that when they bite and do not kill they always leave traces of the venom they have injected.'

Suddenly he whirled Ca-Ca's arm upright. 'Look,' he called clearly. 'To have been bitten by a sand viper would have left a bruise the size of a man's fist. Is there such a bruise — after only three days?'

There was none. That left arm that was supposed to have been bitten was as blameless of blue markings as Ca-Ca's right.

The *chef* spoke from the open doorway, then, where he had been standing with a couple of sergeants for at least two minutes. His heavy blue jowl was lifted truculently; his fleshy mouth had a curl that turned one corner in a sneer of satisfaction; and his brown eyes looked at Ca-Ca, who was beloved of no one, and they boded ill for the man.

The sergeant-major said, '*Mon petit,* there is much in what you have said that interests me. For this, Legionnaire Texas, you will be excused those drills that were given you because of the weakness of your so-long legs.' Then he turned to Ca-Ca, of the bloody face and bruised body, and his voice lifted in passion. 'You, you malingering dog, away to the *cellules* until we have time to consider the punishment your conduct so richly merits!'

And he went away to tell the captain that he, by his cleverness, had seen through Ca-Ca's infamy and had detected him for the rogue he was.

When Ca-Ca had been led away, Tex found his bed surrounded by the quintet. He looked at them quickly. Their mood was murderous, yet he sensed the panic that was in them and he realized that in some way he had interfered with some desperate plan of theirs.

He demanded, 'What d'you want?'

The Bulgar grabbed him by the bare shoulder and pulled him round. 'An end to your blabbing tongue!'

Mervin Petrie had him by the right wrist, and his disease-marked face was passionate. 'Fool, you have talked enough. You have caused enough trouble. There will be no more of it.'

La Femme had him by the other wrist, and he, for all the slightness of his build, was hurting . . . deliberately. Cheauvin came up behind and grabbed Tex by the hair and savagely yanked back his head so that his throat was bared. Tex crashed backwards on to a bed. Quelclos was running across with something in his hand — a knife perhaps. It was a moment of murderous passion, with anything likely to happen. Tex, helpless for the moment, could only think, 'It's something big — an' bad, what they're up to. Takin' Ca-Ca's gummed the works!'

6

Elegant cracked Dwarf Quelclos with the butt of a rifle and sent the half-pint head over heels against a bed. Then he swung the rifle so that it covered the savage little group that had the big Texan sprawled across the bed. His Brooklyn voice yapped, 'I'm gonna start blowin' holes in people's heads. Any guy that fancies a hole in his head, just keep doin' what you're doin'.'

Rube Koskowsci, The Schemer, was alongside him, his eyes bright above his shining red cheeks. His Lebel was clutched to his side, safety-catch off and ready to fire. Dimmy got the idea more slowly, but when it came he remembered that it was over him the row had started, and he wanted to swing at the startled men with his rifle, only Rube shoved him to one side.

Tex, released and dragging himself away from the group, noticed that Louie came in with his rifle later even than Dimmy, and he didn't forget it. Louie of the camel face didn't have much heart for trouble, not other people's troubles, anyway.

Tex was angry. He was also shaken by his nearness to possible death. He saw the ugly little dwarf, getting up slowly from against the wall, and it was a razor the fellow had in his hand. A cut-throat.

He rubbed his head. Cheauvin had hurt, had nearly pulled the hair out of his head. Cheauvin was very close to him. Tex, raging, grabbed the Belgian and ran him against the wall. He hit him a few times with all the strength he had, and then he became disgusted because the fellow wasn't fighting back, and released him.

'Get the hell away from my bed,' he roared, and then the other four men promptly moved.

La Femme went to his bed daintily, as if he were mentally apart from all this violence, but as he reached for his shirt he was thinking, complacently, 'Very well, my friend. But perhaps I know of a way to cook your goose . . . '

It was a bad day for the garrison at Fort El Kwatra. The news that had been brought in, that an attack upon the post was contemplated, made for jitteriness, and men were touchy and quarrelsome. It would be different when the fighting started, but this long waiting, never knowing when an attack might be set up, played on their nerves.

If affected the officers, too. They were more stupid than usual in their handling of the men, and the N.C.O.s amplified their follies and gave the men hell at the least opportunity.

Added to this, it was a day hotter than ordinarily, with a haze of dust occasionally rising and fogging the sun and yet not tempering its heat at all. The sweat ran off men's bodies, but would not evaporate and so cool them.

'We're in for a sirocco,' men said broodingly, yet it wasn't the time for the hot dust storms to begin. Probably, they amended, it would be just a blow-out from the desert, with this rising wind getting hotter and hotter as it raced in from the centre of the Sahara. It would be over in a matter of hours, but while it lasted they would touch the depths of misery.

Life was hard enough in the sun-bleached desert post, without storm winds blowing. Those who could, prayed that their enemies would not add to their discomforts by mounting the expected attack on El Kwatra.

In time, though, Legionnaire Texas, who was wise to the ways of men, began to feel there was more than threats of storms and Arab attacks behind the jitteriness in that post. He tried to analyse the atmosphere, but failed, yet he knew there was something.

It was something that struck at the hearts of men, some instinct that warned of a disaster beyond magnitude . . . of events mounting inexorably that would suddenly envelop and engulf them.

And with it all, Tex suddenly began to realize what it was the men were sensing.

There was treachery afoot.

He looked straight at the Ca-Ca gang at that, for if treachery came it would surely come only through such sweepings of the Continental gutters. But they seemed incapable of doing harm. He dismissed the thought and theory as fanciful. It was ridiculous.

'Peaudezébie,' he found himself saying. How could these trollops, as much prisoners within the fortress ramparts as their comrades, perform any act of treachery? His thoughts idled to Ca-Ca, who was said to have been a Petain man during Vichy, but had worked with the dreaded S.S. Group.

Anything could be expected of that vermin, yet he was immured in the cells and there was little a man could do, for or against anyone, behind those brick walls and heavy bars.

He dismissed the thought, though it kept returning to him. Instead he thought whimsically. 'Holy gee, if I go back to Texas sayin' 'peaudezébie' when I mean, 'The hell, no!' the boys'll sure take the shine outa me.'

Texas . . . A land with plenty of desert, true, but not a desert such as this. Men were free throughout those broad lands, and there were many places where a man could find water himself and horse. Certainly there was no army of mercenaries, no collection of broken men, as here in the Sahara, to defile the country with their very existence. And no days of riding between waterholes as they would find when they risked their lives on that mad scheme of Rube's to gain British territory at Lake Chad in Central Africa.

Each time he thought of that trip, upon which he had promised to go, his mind balked at the responsibility he was undertaking. His comrades' lives were in his hands, yet he was deliberately using them as bait to attract the attentions of the enemy.

If he failed in his plans — failed ultimately, that was, in besting Sturmer — his comrades' lives would be forfeit and they would lose them because he, their comrade whom they trusted, wouldn't go on this trip unless he was quite sure that the *partizans* would follow . . .

All day during duty his mind rebelled at what he was going to do, and yet there was in him something that drove him relentlessly through with this plan which had started in Texas and had brought him all the way to Europe — to Marseilles — then to the Legion.

What had got him worse than anything, though, was the thought that he would be risking the girl's life, too, on that mad escape bid across the mighty Sahara.

When he was free from duty he began to cross the parade ground in an effort to speak with the girl again. This time he would find out her name and what she was doing in French Colonial Africa.

He was trudging along, sweating heavily with the exertion because of that close atmosphere, when he heard his name called. It was Rube.

The Schemer came across in a hurry, as if the oppressive atmosphere didn't affect him. Once again the big Texan marvelled at the enthusiasm and energy in this alert-minded Polish-American. Those red cheeks were perennially boyish, and the gleam in those eyes also spoke of youthful zest and enjoyment. Rube got a kick out of everything he did. It had seemed a good scheme to join the Legion — now

123

it seemed a better one to get out of it and cock a snoot at all the officers, N.C.O.s, *partizans* and military police who insisted that desertion was impossible.

Tex felt his spirits rising when he looked on that bright face. Somehow he felt that this resourceful young American would rise to whatever occasion was required. He shrugged. Well, he would have his chance when it came to smuggling a man out of the country . . . Sturmer.

Rube said, loudly enough only for his ears, 'Brother, I sure fixed it. We go on guard tonight over them damn camels. We'll be on for the next twenty-four hours.'

'All of us.'

Rube looked contemptuous. 'What else? When I fix things, they're fixed good and proper. Sure we're all on. You, me, the kid from Brooklyn, Dimmy who'll play hell because he's just comin' off guard, an' . . .'

'The Camel?'

'Yeah, Louie the Sourpuss.'

Tex studied his shadow. He said, 'Louie gives me the willies. I've got a feeling there's a fellar who c'n let us down.'

Rube said, 'I hate his guts, but you know how it is. Elegant kind of fancies him, because he comes from the next village. He won't believe the fellar's poison. Says it's just an inferiority complex because the guy wasn't born in Brooklyn.'

'Where'n hell that guy gets all them long words,' said Tex and then he said, abruptly, 'Look, pardner, tell Louie he's on guard, but don't tell him you fixed things or what's behind it.'

Rube wasn't laughing now. His blue eyes were fixed on Texas. He trusted the ex-puncher's hunches more than he trusted anyone's, and what the big fellar said went with him.

'You figger he might get cold feet and talk an' bust things up for us?' The Schemer went cold at the idea.

Texas shrugged. 'I don't know. But I say, don't take chances. We'll tell Louie what's givin' at the moment we're about to make the break. If he wants to come he c'n come. If he seems kinda stuck on Fort El Kwatra . . . '

Rube said, 'Yeah?' grimly.

'We'll hog-tie him, so he can't go yammerin' before we're out of the district.'

The Schemer nodded approvingly. Then he said, 'This means we've got to take food an' water today, so we c'n move out on them camels after dark. That'll give us a night's start. I'll fix that. Bein' on guard tonight means we c'n go in an' out the post a few times without arousin' suspicion . . . '

Tex nodded. He too was planning. He looked round. Nobody seemed to be observing them. He said, 'Me, I've got to smuggle an Ay-rab an' a girl out through them gates. That'll take some doing.'

The problem excited Rube's active mind. 'You just hold your hosses for a minute, cowboy,' he promised, 'an' I'll up with a humdinger of a scheme for you.'

Tex grinned. 'I figger I c'n cook up my own scheme,' he said. 'Now — scram, buddy!'

Texas strolled over to where the Arabs were sullenly encamped in the shadow of the high wall. Some greeted him, perhaps knowing that he had helped their wounded brother Arab, but even the greeting was restrained. These Arabs were very worried men.

Tex watched them. A few were playing a desultory game with little stones on a series of squares traced out with a finger on the hot sand. But most were just squatting, enveloped in their white burnouses, like a lot of white crows, Tex thought.

He hitched his thumbs into his belt and strolled off between the tents. Souriya, or whatever her real name was, must have been on the look out for him. She called, yet only loud enough for him to hear, 'Hello, Longfellow.'

He edged towards the tent, his eyes, under the pulled-down brim of his kepi, watching quickly in all directions. There were a few men about, but they were lounging in the shade of the central blockhouse, where Ca-Ca languished in the cells. A few more men were by the barrack rooms, but they also seemed occupied with everything except the Arabs by the big wall.

He heard the girl's voice again, 'Come round to the back, Tex. Step right into the tent, brother; I want to talk with you.'

He ambled round. His heart was beating faster. Now he would have the chance to see what sort of a face matched those blue eyes. A crack appeared in the wall of the tent. Tex saw a movement and walked inside.

There was plenty of light inside, yet after the glare of the sun on the parade ground, it took seconds for Tex's eyes to adjust themselves. When they did, he saw carpets, soft cushions — there was colour and brightness and the hands of women everywhere.

Then he saw the women, and he was surprised — almost shocked. There were four in the tent, and three were Arab girls.

They stood back from him, clinging together, and obviously terrified behind their *yashmaks,* yet with it all delighted. This was certainly the first time in their lives that an infidel had entered their tent.

Tex saw high, brown cheekbones, saw lovely soft, gazelle-like brown eyes. There was a scent of rose essence and the soft, alluring sound of clinging, silken robes rusting . . .

He looked at the fourth girl. She was laughing at him. She was wearing her *houri* costume, but the *yashmak* was gone. He saw a round, honey-brown face that wasn't in the least Arabic; saw white, even teeth that gleamed and reflected highlights as she laughed; saw those soft red lips that he hadn't been able to think about, and they were as inviting as he'd hoped them to be.

She smiled, laughter dancing in her blue eyes, and said, mockingly, 'Welcome to our harem, O Infidel.' He couldn't tear his eyes away from her blonde beauty, though the Arab maidens were good enough to attract his attention at any other time.

She held out her hand. 'No kidding,' she said, 'my real name's Monica Shaw. Generally known as Nicky Shaw where I work.'

Hanging on a tent pole was a whole cluster of expensive photographic equipment. Tex gave a guess, 'You're from a noospaper.'

She agreed. 'I'm from a noospaper. A Noo York one, Texas.' She wasn't laughing now, but looked businesslike — bonny but calculating.

He could take his eyes away from her now, and they looked towards the Arab girls. He met warm, bright, brown ones that fluttered and faltered and dropped but then quickly returned to meet his. He might have the Evil Eye, but these girls were willing to risk a lot to have a look at a strange man, Tex thought ironically. He gave a wink and a click of his tongue and that set them to giggling.

Nicky said, 'Keep your eyes off those girls, soldier. They're being very daring, letting you visit us. If their men folk knew . . . '

Tex shoved back his kepi. It was hotter than hell inside this tent, yet the girls seemed cool enough. He wondered why it was that girls never felt the heat the same as men.

He said, 'There's a big penalty for takin' photographs in this zone. The French don't like foreign reporters nosin' around the Legion posts.' He asked, 'Is that why you came?'

She hesitated. 'Maybe.' she said. 'I

wanted a special ... photograph.' She turned the subject slightly. 'That's why I came through with a friendly Arab caravan.' She didn't say she had been across that desert twice before with caravans, but just hadn't had any luck on the first occasions.

Tex grunted, 'Jeepers, if they knew ... ' The authorities would go screaming mad if they found a foreign reporter within the walls of a military fort, especially one with a camera.

Tex said, 'Honey, it's fixed for us to move out tonight.'

'Us?' Her eyes were shining. 'You going?' He nodded. She said, quickly, 'I'm glad, Tex. I feel I can trust you. Those others ... ' She shrugged.

He looked round but failed to see the wounded Arab. 'Where's Achmet the Seedy?'

'The men put him in another tent where they could look after him. That's why *les girls* dropped in to keep me company.'

He was thinking, 'Very nice, too.' But brought his thoughts and eyes back to business. 'Honey, each night some Arabs are permitted to go out and give water to their camels. Can you fix for you an' Achmet to go with the party, dressed as male Ay-rabs?'

'I think it can be fixed. We don't come back, is that the idea? Won't they notice — and what about the guard on the camels?' Her blue eyes were suddenly apprehensive.

'We're the guard — me an' some boys from Brooklyn Bronx, an' other places in God's own country. We're goin' on pump with you tonight. Get through them gates, an' you'll be okay, baby.'

The smile came back to her eyes, but she said, 'Less of the baby talk, brother. And see none of your *poumpists* get wrong ideas, will you?'

'I'll see they don't,' the big Texan said, and there was such vehemence in his voice that her eyes suddenly dropped.

He looked round again for the last time. The Arab girls giggled and flashed their teeth in smiles and dropped their eyes but again lifted them quickly so that they didn't miss anything.

The girl was peeping out through the opening to the rear of the tent. She whispered, 'There's no one about, not at the back here, anyway. Goodbye until tonight, then.'

He whispered, 'Until tonight — honey,' and quickly stepped out into the sunshine. His heart was beating faster at the thought of the days ahead . . .

When he turned the end of the tent to cross the parade ground, he found himself confronted by the girl-like Legionnaire who was known as La Femme.

With him was Cheauvin the Belgian. Mervin Petrie, Dwarf Quelclos and the Bulgar.

And with them almost every man in the post was standing silently there, waiting until he came out of the tent.

7

Startled, Tex came to a halt so suddenly that he seemed to rock on his heels. He saw eyes straining towards him, saw inflamed passion on the faces of these men who had had to live like celibates most of their lives. They reminded him of hungry-eyed wolves — and just as dangerous.

His eyes flickered towards La Femme. He didn't need to be told what had happened. This was revenge for getting their leader tossed into the cooler. La Femme had suspected something, the previous day, and he must have been watching from a distance.

When Tex disappeared he must have gone round the barrack rooms, perhaps telling the Legionnaires that there were Arab maidens who were willing to talk with men, for was not one of their number inside one of the tents right at that moment?

Perhaps he had added that the favours of one man might be available to others, if they wished. And at that there would have been a stampede across towards the tents.

At which moment Tex must have come out.

The silence was broken by a sudden roar from those throats before him. The mob simultaneously surged towards the tents where the womenfolk were. Some of the women, watching through cracks in their tents, must have seen the movement and correctly interpreted it, for they began to scream in fear.

The Arabs, who had been lounging alongside the high wall, came running round at once. There were about thirty Arabs, and they had no arms other than sticks and knives, but in defence of their womenfolk they placed themselves before that oncoming mob of Legionnaires.

Someone shouted, 'Trample on those dogs of Arabs!'

A roar of approval went up from the excited men. They charged on to the Arabs, fists and feet going. Screaming that this was the treachery they had expected from the murderous infidels, the Arabs fought like cats against superior numbers.

Dust rose under the scuffling feet. The air was hideous with the sound of savage, fighting men — the thud of fists upon flesh, of boots upon bony legs, the swearing of the many tongued Legionnaires and the war cries of the Mohammedans.

Tex stood back against the tent wherein was the American girl. His eyes were blazing. He wasn't going to let this scum get near that girl. Some Legionnaires broke through the cordon of struggling Arabs. One was the Bulgar. Of course the Bulgar would be the first man through.

Tex hit him and knocked him back among the fighters. Then he jumped at the other men, fury gripping his soul. His fists smashed at them, one blow only per man. He saw one man go down, his face contorting with pain he had never imagined; saw another cover his face and go staggering to one side out of the fighting. Then a third lost all interest in the affray.

Tex was fighting berserk. As men

crashed through the line of Arabs, those mighty fists pounded them back again.

Savage shouts assailed his ears as the Legionnaires saw who stood between them and the prizes. The soldiers redoubled their efforts and the Arabs went under, engulfed by the wave of mercenaries. Tex found himself facing a hundred furious men. His face snarled defiance and his fists lifted to give them all he had before he, too, went under, as indeed he knew he would.

For one second it seemed that the man and the mob stood motionless, facing each other. Then the first movement was begun, a man began to run forward, shouting in triumph.

La Femme, of course, who let others do the fighting, but was always to hand when the prizes came up.

He never reached those tents. A roar of sound filled the parade ground within those high walls. Rock splinters were gouged from the big defence wall, just above the tents and just below the catwalks along which the sentries stood.

Men halted as if petrified, then turned

to see the author of all this sound.

It was Captain Anton Duvet, magnificent in his be-medalled uniform, a sneer on his lips as he surveyed them. By his side was a Legionnaire who had blasted out those warning rounds from a hastily dragged up machine-gun.

Deathly silence followed, broken only by the groans of the injured who pulled themselves staggeringly to their feet. Then the high-pitched, cynical voice of the fort commander demanded, 'Is it that you are all bitten by the beetle *cafard*? What has happened? Who started this? Is it a riot or a war between Arabs and soldiers?'

He swaggered about, confident that he had the situation under control, as indeed he had. He pointed to a Legionnaire. 'You, dog, tell me who started this?'

So the man told him, because it was Dwarf Quelclos, who could say no good of any man. 'It was the swaggering Legionnaire from the land of the almighty dollar,' he said, his thick lips mouthing the words as though he liked them.

'*Le Legionnaire Texas* has found his way into the Arab women's tents, and it is the opinion of these men that where one can go, all can go.'

'And you were in the act of going, when their Arab men-folk intervened!' Suddenly he let his temper ride out unbridled. He looked at the cowering, half-dressed, bloody-faced men, and he screamed with rage. 'You fools, you sons of disease-ridden she asses! Must I have my parade ground turned into a shambles? Must I have you disabling yourselves perhaps only hours before the dreaded Abdul el Nuhas attacks this post as it has never been attacked before?'

'Go to your quarters, you scum, you lower than dogs. For this you will assuredly find punishment when I can consider what way it shall be imposed.' His tongue crept out and licked his lips. In his way he was enjoying this bout of anger. He was also enjoying the thought of punishing these men. It was good to have an excuse to inflict punishment on men at times . . .

Then he turned his bright, brown eyes on to the Legionnaire Texas. He rapped out an order, and to half a dozen listening people it was like the voice of doom.

'Into the cells with that wretch who began all this trouble. He will learn not to go where he should not go,' he shouted.

For one second Tex's hands doubled and came up as if he would fight the escort that came racing from the guard-room to take him to the cells. For this meant failure to his plans; he would not be able to go with them on the breakout that night.

Utter frustration and fury gripped him at the thought. Rube had fixed them on the camel guard and they could get away that night and take the girl and the wounded Arab with them. But if they didn't make the break that night, they would probably not again get a chance to desert so easily, certainly not before the discovery of the wanted Arab and this girl with her cameras in a military zone. He was less worried about what the authori- ties would do with her if she were discovered than with the danger from some of these wild, unruly Legionnaires.

His hands dropped to his sides. It was no use fighting; the odds were too great.

His eyes flickered towards the tent whose occupants had been saved only by his ferocity in defending it. A curtain fluttered. Nicky Shaw, American news reporter, was watching him, perhaps suffering with him, he thought. Well, she wouldn't suffer what he would suffer in those damn' cells, he told himself.

He passed through among the men, who treated him with hostility. That was unusual. Apart from the fact that he was quite a popular Legionnaire, generally for a man to be carted off to the cells earned for him a passionate sympathy and warmth of unaccustomed friendliness from his embittered, authority-hating comrades.

But these men felt a grudge against him. He had gone where they all wanted to go, within those womens' tents, and then he had stood in their way and made such a scene that he had brought the officers on to them. The Arabs? They shrugged. They could have handled those. But now they were to receive punishment at the hands of that grinning popinjay of a captain.

Tex gave back glare for glare. He wasn't to be intimidated by any of them. If it came to a stand-up fight, he felt capable of dealing with any pair of them . . . right then, in that awful rage of his, he felt mad enough to handle any six of them!

It was a bad day for Tex in that tiny cell. It measured six feet by four feet only, and was barely six feet high, so that there was little comfort for him whether he lay down on the bare plank bed or stood up.

It was whitewashed and dry — too dry — and the sun blazed intolerably through the unshaded barred opening that served as a window and ventilator to the cell. The door was of thick wood, with one small, barred observation hatch through which the guard outside could periodically inspect the prisoners and see that they were not doing anything silly — such as hanging themselves with their belts.

Restless, Tex kept walking over to that hatch in the door, to look at the guardroom beyond. Generally there was the guard corporal and three or four off-duty guards sitting around a trestle table, or lying on their blankets in a corner and dozing.

Once he saw Dimmy, who was on guard still, but the American didn't look his way and went out. But when the evening meal of soup and bread was brought to him, it was Dimmy who carried the cans.

Dimmy hissed through the hatch, 'The fellars want to know what to do tonight, Tex?' Then he opened the door and shoved the cans just within reach and slammed the door again. The corporal was watching from his table.

'Tell 'em to go,' Tex whispered back promptly, while Dimmy wrestled with an apparently refractory key outside. 'You too, Dimmy. Them camels outside give you a better than usual chance of gettin' away. The Ay-rab an' the gal will be out by now, I figger, hidin' up near the camels.'

Sure he'd come after them. Nothing would keep him back, once he was able to get over that damn' wall. He'd move heaven and earth to catch up with them, because the *partizans* and their vicious leader would be hot on the trail of the deserters within a matter of hours. He wanted to be with his comrades when Sturmer caught up with them. He had to be . . . that would be the moment he had worked and waited for for years now.

Dimmy went. Tex was left alone all evening. Evidently the captain didn't feel inclined to try to punish him that day, but would leave it for his morning defaulters' parade. Tex resigned himself to a night in the cell. It wasn't, after all, much worse than lying in the barrack room. Stuffier, perhaps, and with more creeping things to keep him company, but that was all.

He stood at his barred window and looked out wherever there was light. The Arabs were still among their tents; blue-tunicked Legionnaires moved occasionally across the hot, dusty parade ground. But mostly everything was quiet — so quiet that the occasional flapping of the tricolour, high up on the mast, could be heard by the prisoners.

He saw the lengthening shadows, the gathering purple gloom over the vast, yellow desert, and he wondered what was happening beyond the gates, where the

Arabs' camels were tethered.

His comrades would be 'guarding' them, theoretically, patrolling with ready rifles in case of an attempted breakout by the unfortunate Arabs inside the post, or in case of desert thieves from the world beyond.

The Arab and Nicky would be lying up near them, all ready to move just as soon as the night shadows were dark enough. He thought, 'Good luck. May your trails be short and easy . . . ' And he found himself saying it in Arabic — a conventional saying among his comrades, and he wondered yet again what reception he would have if he greeted trail herders in faraway Texas in a foreign tongue. Probably within weeks he would have forgotten these words that came so naturally to his lips now . . .

He heard Ca-ca's voice. He had forgotten that the renegade was in jail with him. His ears pricked and he swung round, away from the gloom of night through the window, and looked at the yellow oil light in the guardroom beyond.

Ca-ca was talking. It was a quick,

hurried conversation, kept so low that Tex was unable to hear what was being said.

Stealthily he tiptoed to the barred hatch set in the door. He saw that the corporal of the guard was absent from the table. It would be the new guard, of course, taking over at sundown. Two men were standing by the door that led out on to the parade ground. They were standing in the tense attitudes of men watching. One turned, so that the yellow light from the solitary oil lamp fell full on his face.

It wept. It was the Belgian, Cheauvin, the Weeper.

Then the second man turned. It was the former assistant to the guillotiner at Marseilles, Mervin Petrie.

Tex pressed his face to the bars, trying to see who it was who spoke with Ca-ca. At that moment Petrie whispered, 'Look out!' and he and The Weeper leapt to the trestle table, so that when the corporal came in they had all the appearance of men immersed in a game of cards.

The third guard just as hurriedly joined them in their game. It was La Femme.

Tex went and sat on his plank bed and

146

did some thinking. Minutes later when he looked again into the guardroom, it was to see Dwarf Quelclos there — and then the Bulgar, his face bruised from the battering of Tex's fists, came lurching in from the parade ground.

All Ca-ca's gang were on guard.

Tex thought, 'That's some coincidence!' As much a coincidence as that which had provided an all-American guard for the camels that night.

The Legionnaire from Texas knew at once that some wangling had been contrived. The Ca-ca mob had fixed things to be on this guard all together, just as Rube had fixed things with regard to the camel guard. But why? Tex could only think, 'It's somethin' to do with Ca-ca. Ca-ca ain't gonna stay a prisoner much longer, I guess!'

And he found himself grinning. Clearly the Ca-ca gang were planning to go on pump, he thought. That only could be the explanation of this intrigue. And he thought, 'They've fixed to use some of them camels outside. Wal, they're gonna be downright disappointed!'

For Rube had planned to take what camels he needed, and to turn the rest adrift so that their tracks obscured the ones the *poumpists* made.

He went back to his plank bed and lay there for a while, curled up awkwardly on its hard narrowness because he was too long for it. He tried to think what was happening out with the camels.

By now Nicky and the wounded Arab would have joined the Americans; Louie the Camel would have been dealt with if he got scared of going on pump; and right now the little party should be moving out . . .

The daytime sounds around the post gradually died as men settled down to their beds or night duties along the ramparts. Shortly before midnight the only sound that Tex could hear was the cough of the guard corporal who was trying to keep awake in the sultry heat by smoking continuously. Moroccan tobacco wasn't good for chain-smoking.

Tex, thinking about his fleeing comrades, found himself unable to sleep. He also had some vague inner feeling of disquiet, as if instinct told him of disaster so closely ahead.

He was alert then, when he heard the scrape of feet on the sandy floor of the guardroom ... heard a dull thud, followed by a long, drawn-out sigh that was almost a moan.

Immediately there was a quick scurry of feet, and a sharp exclamation. Tex came to his feet and went across to the barred hatch in the door.

He looked out, and gasped. The corporal was down on the floor, as if he had fallen asleep and toppled from his chair.

But Tex knew he hadn't fallen asleep. There was blood pooling by his black hair.

Tex saw the Bulgar standing over him, bad teeth showing in a mirthless grin as he looked down on the stricken, dying man. In his hand was a heavy metal bayonet scabbard.

Mervin Petrie was almost across to the next-door cell, in his hands the heavy ring and big keys that fitted the doors. He was lost to sight for a second, during which time Tex heard the key rattle in the lock. Then Ca-ca stepped into view.

He looked bruised about the face, all puffed up and ugly from the battering he had received at Tex's hands that morning. But something important must have obsessed his thoughts, for he didn't so much as look at the cell in which his enemy lay. Instead he ran quickly, but on tiptoe, towards the guard-room door. The Bulgar followed as far as the doorway, and then stood still, rifle in hand as if mounting guard over the silent guard-room.

Tex licked his lips. He thought of shouting, of giving warning; because it was a wretched thing to do, to strike down a man unaware of danger from his comrades. But the Bulgar in the doorway kept Tex's tongue silent. Maybe in a few minutes the Bulgar would take his rifle and go, and Tex could kick up a fuss and bring help to that badly injured corporal lying on the floor.

He tiptoed back to the window. He could see quite easily now, because a desert moon was riding high, and he looked on a ghostly world of cold, white light and the blackest of black shadows.

A group of dark figures were flitting quickly across to where the big gate was. As he watched, he saw two of them operate the mechanism, which lifted the gate. Surprised, he realized it was rising without any sound. Usually the creak and groans of the windlass could be heard in every corner of the post. He thought; 'Someone's been greasing the windlass.' That someone would be one of Ca-ca's gang, of course.

He was bewildered, though. Why should deserters open the main gate in order to make their getaway? It wouldn't have hurt them to have hung over the outside of the wall and dropped into the soft sand below. And it would have been much quicker. But that little group of figures stood crouching on either side of the lifting gate that began to show as a light patch against the blackness of the shadowy wall.

He heard the Bulgar suddenly leave the guardroom, and then saw his figure as he joined the men at the gate. And the gate was rising slowly . . .

Tex's hands suddenly gripped those bars as if he would wrench them from their sockets. His eyes widened with incredulity and horror. He couldn't believe what he saw; he thought. 'Oh, God, this is a dream! This isn't possible! Men can't be as low as all that!'

But they were. Ca-ca and his men were committing the vilest act that Tex had ever known. That is, all except one other crime . . .

For now Tex could see through the opening gate. Could look out on to the moonlit desert beyond.

And he saw horsemen.

Hundreds of them.

And they were jogging forward in steady procession, four abreast, riding straight towards the gate that gave them access to the fort.

They were Arabs.

8

Tex dived for the door and kicked it savagely, as if he would batter it down with his heavy boots, and his voice raised in a bellow of warning.

'To arms! To arms! It is the Arabs!'

The effect of his voice and the mighty pounding of boots upon resounding door must have wakened the fortress in an instant. All over the post, men leapt from their beds and seized rifles and came out running. The shout, 'To arms!' was taken up on all sides, until the place echoed with the cry.

But it was too late. The crime had been committed; the tragedy was about to begin.

Tex raced back to the window to see the effect of his warning upon the approaching Arab army. They were spurring in through the gateway, opened to them by the traitors. Tex saw the white-robed Arab horsemen pour onto the parade ground in an all-engulfing flood, He thought he saw Ca-ca and his men slip out onto the desert beyond, and it seemed they were given safe passage at that . . .

In that moment he understood the lot. That viper — that supposed snake bite that had sent Ca-ca staggering off into the desert — it was all part of this plan.

Ca-ca was playing traitor again; not for nothing was he regarded as a renegade against his country.

He had used that viper to provide him with an excuse for a couple of days' absence, during which time he must have contacted the Arab leaders — perhaps the mighty Abdul el Nuhas himself — and put this plan of handing over the Legion post of El Kwatra to them. No doubt he and his comrades would get riches and safe passage out of the country.

Tex cursed them for the blackest of villains. To desert was one thing; to give your comrades to the enemy as part of the plan to desert was another — and reprehensible.

Almost from the moment he reached the window again, he realized that the

Legionnaires didn't stand a chance. There were too many Arabs, and they were packing the parade ground before the men had time to get out from the barrack rooms.

The crash of rifle fire filled the night with ugly, ragged sound. Everywhere flames spat into the darkness, hurling deadly, spinning lead at each other. Tex got the stink of cordite in his nose, and it seemed to drive him crazy. He was cooped up inside this cell, without a chance of defending himself. When the Arabs won — as they must win — he knew they would come in and cut him down and that was no sort of death to contemplate with calmness.

The Arabs were screaming their war cries now, milling around with swords uplifted, charging little groups of half-wakened Legionnaires and cutting them down by sheer weight of numbers. It was nightmarish, that scene — the cries of the tormented and dying, the savagery of men crazed by blood lust, hacking and killing, and being hacked and killed in return.

Tex wheeled back to the door and kicked into it again. He was shouting, 'Let me out of here! For God's sake come an' open this damned door!' In fury he shook it, but it was too strong for that treatment.

Then a Legionnaire came running into the room and grabbed the machine-gun, ready on its tripod in a corner. He picked it up, cursing and sweating. He was a Latvian, big, black-browed and morose. But a comrade.

When he saw Tex helpless there, he took precious time off to grab the keys from the lock of Ca-ca's former cell and release the American. Then, swearing savagely, he stooped again to pick up that heavy machine-gun.

Tex grabbed him by the arm, though, and stopped him.

'That's no good,' he shouted frantically. 'It's too late!'

He kicked the door to and dropped the heavy bar. That shut out the frenzied scene in the moonlit parade ground, but didn't cut out the sound. It sounded like a thousand madmen all screaming and shouting at once, all equipped with some means of making further noise, such as guns or sabres that crashed against each other . . .

Tex worked like mad. He grabbed a kepi for himself; tossed a full *bidon* to the Latvian and then slung a water bottle across his own back. It was no good escaping death at the hands of the Arabs, only to meet one equally as painful out in the arid desert.

He grabbed a Lebel and some ammunition, then raced into the back passage that led into the blockhouse. There was a ladder along the passage that gave access to the roof. The Latvian suddenly understood and came hard after him as he started to climb.

On the roof Tex saw other figures. They were Legionnaires who had also seen the futility of making a stand and were escaping across the flat roofs.

Tex heard hoarse breathing as he jumped for the floorboards that made up the catwalk against the fortress walls. He heaved and pulled himself up, then bent over and grabbed the Latvian and

157

dragged him alongside him. Then he ran along the catwalk and helped up a couple of comrades who hadn't the strength to get up unaided. One seemed to be wounded, for he cried out when Tex pulled on his shoulder.

More men were coming up through the various traps on to the roof of the blockhouse, and then Tex saw the first of the Arabs to come rushing up after them. The Latvian had his rifle up in a flash and sent the Arab reeling down the steps he had just ascended.

Tex leapt for an embrasure in the thick wall and pulled himself through. Behind him the mad slaughter raged: he looked down upon a swaying, swirling mass of men — realized that most were Arab dressed, and there was little firing of Lebels now. The betrayal of Fort El Kwatra was nearly complete.

He wanted to get away from that scene of carnage, wanted to rid his ears of those sounds of men screaming their last agonies while the big, beautiful moon shone coldly, brilliantly down upon the struggle.

Swiftly he turned and lowered himself over the wall, still gripping his Lebel, and then he let himself go and felt himself dropping through space. He let his limbs go slack as he hit soft sand, and went over backwards, somersaulting to break the force of the landing. Someone else thudded into the sand a few yards away.

He heard the voice of the *Chef*. 'Keep together, my children. Together we might fight our way to freedom!'

Might! Anyway, Tex couldn't stick with the sergeant-major and the others, because he had to go after the deserters.

He looked at the stars and struck off across the yielding sandy desert. The moon was so bright that he could easily see the way he was going. Southeast of him more Arabs were racing across towards the fortress. Many were on foot. He thought, 'No one'll take much notice of me for a while.' And he walked swiftly, openly, upright.

A few minutes later he found himself climbing a rocky tongue that ended in a short cliff. Just as he came there he saw horsemen racing towards him, heading for the fort. He thought, 'Goldarn it, I need a hoss!' He stood erect on the cliff edge, daring recognition as the hard-riding Arabs rushed eagerly along to join in the battle. Perhaps because he was motionless they never saw him.

He saw the leaders go by, then the main group. Then he saw a lone horseman rapidly overtaking them and he decided this was his man. When the horse and rider drew level he launched himself off the bluff with all the force he could out into the dive.

It was something he had done many times before at rodeos and on the range. But always before it had been in sport, and it had been in daylight. The moon was big and bright, but still a long way from giving the same light as the sun.

Yet Tex timed it beautifully. His shoulder crashed the Arab right out of his saddle, had him floored before he could so much as yell out. Tex went over on to the ground after him carried by the force of his dive, but he was curling his legs round, so that he landed running, and his hand grabbed for the mane of that startled little Arab pony and held it.

The pony tried to rear away, but ran only into the wall of the bluff. Tex's long legs took enormous strides, frantically holding on to that mane, and then he got his other hand on to the ornamented saddle and in a flash he had recovered his balance and was vaulting on to the pony's back.

From that moment there was no bother. In the saddle, Tex was at home. He looked again at the stars, then turned his pony southwards and went at a steady gallop after the *poumpists*.

They would have a few hours start of him, but though a camel moved at a deceptively fast speed, he knew he would catch up with his comrades by dawn.

He had ridden for about a quarter of an hour, so that all sounds of the battle had died in his ears, when he saw the red glow reflecting in the sky. He turned in the saddle.

From that distance he was able to watch the end of Fort El Kwatra. The Arabs had fired it, and now it was burning furiously. They would have taken all the arms and ammunition they wanted, and now were ensuring that never again would the fortress be employed against them.

Tex shrugged. He was cynical. It wasn't his fort, and he had no good opinion of the French way of administering Arab territory. So long as he attained his own objective, he didn't give a hang how many forts were burned down by the Arabs. Legionnaire Texas had no illusions now about the Foreign Legion — if he'd ever had any.

The one thought that worried him was — those flames could be seen for fifty miles around. It might bring the *partizans* up. He wanted to meet up with them, or rather their leader but he wanted it in his own time, when he was ready. When he was with his comrades and able to achieve the daring plan he had so desperately embarked upon.

He also wondered if the whole affair — the rising of the Arabs against their tyrannical masters — mightn't upset his plans. Perhaps it would take Sturmer's interest off deserters for a while, and it

162

was vitally important that that should not happen. More than anything in the world he wanted Sturmer to come after him. If necessary with his ferocious headhunters, but certainly to come after him.

Almost he prayed that would happen.

He needn't have worried. He was captured by Sturmer within a few minutes of day breaking.

He seemed to ride out of the night in a matter of yards, so quickly did the sun come up on the Sahara. One moment he could see only a limited distance ahead. The next, his vision could take in the horizon, ten miles before him.

And Sturmer and his *partizans* were riding swiftly northwards, right across his track. It was sheer bad luck. He was going south and they were going north, and it was fated that they had to pass each other.

Tex saw that it was too late to try to hide. One of the *partizans* was already shouting and pointing in his direction. At once Sturmer, a Legion officer save for his Arab headdress, changed his course slightly and pounded towards him. His cut-throat gang seemed to close in upon their leader, as if in anticipation of brutal pleasure at sight of that lone Legionnaire where no Legionnaire should be.

Sturmer reined across his path. Deliberately Tex rode up to the ex-Nazi officer. It seemed to the American that the *partizan* leader hunched slightly in his saddle when he recognized him. His head seemed to lower as if to help him peer the more closely through those rimless glasses.

Tex saluted, his face stony to hide his feelings at sight of this man who had brought him, though Sturmer didn't know it, halfway across the world and to a suffering that he'd never contemplated.

Sturmer rapped, 'Where are you going. Legionnaire?' And then he asked, 'What was that fire we saw in the night? Was it El Kwatra?'

Tex said. 'It was El Kwatra.' Because there was no need to hide the truth from this man, though he was his enemy, he told him, 'Six men conspired together and permitted the Ay-rabs to steal into the fortress while they were on guard. The garrison didn't stand a chance. There were too many attackers — and many of our men were probably killed before they could get to their weapons.'

'Some escaped? Like yourself?' Sturmer was watching him with a kind of brooding closeness, as if testing the truth of each statement.

'Maybe a dozen. I saw Sergeant-Major Ransconsi an' a few others drop over the wall. I don't know what happened to the others.'

'You should have kept together, all of you,' said Sturmer harshly, but fortunately he didn't pursue that subject. Instead he demanded, 'Why were you heading south, away from the coast garrisons?'

'The Ay-rabs were in force to the north of the post,' Tex told him, which was true enough.

Sturmer sat his horse in silence after that, his eyes downcast behind those cissy glasses he wore. At last he spoke again, musingly, meditatively. 'And they burnt the fortress down after looting it. They would do that, these dogs of desert scavengers,' he ended savagely. He seemed to get into a rage at the temerity of the Arabs in attacking the Legion post. 'They shall know discipline for this,' he almost shouted. 'Their villages will burn and their people will suffer all over the land. They will learn not to destroy military property — they will be taught the lesson of attacking soldiers!'

That was a true Nazi officer speaking. The army was sacred. No one must do anything against it. And if they did, they would suffer a thousandfold. Tex thought, 'God help these Arabs if men like Sturmer are given the job of handling this situation.'

Then Sturmer's temper left him. Tex realized that he was looking at him, that queer, calculating expression on his thin, curiously pale face under that fluttering Arab headdress.

Sturmer demanded, 'What is your name? Your real name?'

Tex felt himself stiffening. His grey, slitted eyes met the officer's levelly, without yielding. He replied, almost coldly, 'Legionnaire Hank Texas.'

'Bah!' Sturmer shifted quickly, impatiently in his saddle. 'I want your real name. It is . . . Davidson, yes?'

Tex said, 'It is Texas,' though it wasn't. Sturmer had given him his true name.

Sturmer just ignored that reiteration. Instead he shoved his head forward, rather in the manner of a shortsighted tortoise peering, Tex thought. His eyes seemed to be looking for the slightest weakness, for any clue that would enable him to know the truth.

'There was a man I once knew. He was a major in the American Army, at the time when the Germany Army was being forced out of North Africa. He was Major John Davidson. If you're not Davidson, then you're his double — perhaps a brother.'

Then it was that Legionnaire Texas, who could usually control his temper under the most trying of circumstances, lost his head. Suddenly he didn't give a damn if this fiend did know his identity. He had a feeling, anyway, that he had lost — he had fallen into Sturmer's hands, and there was no escape from him and his dreaded *partizans.*

It wasn't in his nature, either, to be

meek and mild, and he rebelled at having to play a role of deception before the man he hated. So he snarled, suddenly, 'So what? Sure I'm a Davidson. Major John was my brother — my twin. I was in Africa, too, at the time — but in hospital, suffering from wounds. Otherwise. I might have gone out with Johnny.'

Sturmer stiffened at the raging tone. And then a look of triumph came to his thin, pale face with its glinting, reflecting glasses that seemed to wipe out any eyes the man might have. It was the triumph of a man who can do bad things to an enemy; he was going to enjoy what followed to this Legionnaire, and his mind was already planning. Not too quickly, of course . . .

'You are in the Legion for a purpose?'

Tex didn't disguise it. 'Yeah, I joined for a reason.'

'Me?'

'You.'

Sturmer gave a signal, and the cavalcade began to move northwards, slowly. Tex had to wheel his horse and ride with them. His Lebel was snatched out of his hands.

Sturmer kept his eyes on him. Tex saw the butt of a military pistol not unlike a Colt protruding from a holster on the officer's thigh. The hold-down strap was buttoned back, as if Sturmer wore his gun on the ready, for instant use.

'You came back to the desert to kill me?'

'Nope.' Sturmer didn't believe him. 'I came to get you an' take you back for trial for what you did at the Pit of Hell.'

Still Sturmer didn't believe him. 'How could you . . . this is nonsense you talk, my friend.'

Tex shrugged indifferently. It wasn't important what was believed. His thoughts were on escape — escape and, ultimately, realization of his plans. And those plans were, as he said, to take Sturmer and hand him over to justice for his crimes against man.

For why should he, Hank Davidson, alone take revenge, when there were thousands who had as much right as he to try and punish this fiend?

His eyes swiftly scanned the desert. Already the air above it was distorting as

169

the blazing sun stirred up hot air currents from the yellow-white sands. He saw rolling sand dunes as far as the eye could see to the north and east and west. Just sand, with an occasional patch of scrub grass or hardy thorn bush.

Escape? There wasn't a chance, he thought bitterly.

Even without the knowledge that he was John Davidson's brother, Sturmer had known, because of the way he was heading, that he was trying to desert. Retribution would be the same — because he was Davidson's brother, and because he was trying to desert.

Tex looked at the sword hilts that protruded from the cloaks of the burnoused men cantering alongside him, and tried not to think of the sharp blade that would come whistling down towards his unprotected neck . . .

Sturmer, musingly, brought the subject back to the Pit of Hell. 'What do you know of that place you just mentioned?'

'All the world knows about it.' Tex found he could talk unemotionally, even before the author of that foul crime. 'The

War Crimes Commission has been looking for you for the past eight years, Sturmer.'

'Sturmer?' That head came round like a vicious, striking snake. The pale face was raging. 'You are a soldier, and I am an officer, *schweinhund*. You will address me as *capitaine*.' Almost, Sturmer was trembling at the way he had been addressed. To his Nazi mind there were two kinds of people in the world — the officer class — and scum!

Deliberately Tex said, 'The hell with your *capitaine*. To me you're Sturmer, a louse who should be squashed out of existence.' His eyes were on that revolver butt. If he was going to die, he'd change his plans. No more high-faluting ideas about handing over this felon to justice. He'd take Sturmer with him, if he could.

Only Sturmer was riding too far away for him to dive for that gun.

Sturmer reined back his horse, so that it reared and opened its mouth in pain at the vicious drag on its bit. The cavalcade stopped. The renegade Arabs came hustling round, sharp eyes interpreting the rage of their officer and sensing action. It was the kind of action they delighted in apart from the bounty it brought, there was the savage thrill that their cruelty brought them.

But Tex faced them all, and wouldn't soften his tone. He was blazing mad, his brown fists clenched — yet helpless.

'Goddamn you,' he snarled, 'you killed my brother, an' a thousand helpless men. You like killin' men, don't you Sturmer? It's your trade, isn't it? Killin'. An' you're still at it aren't you? A butcher, that's what you are.'

Sturmer had control of himself now. He knew the cards were stacked in his favour; this impudent Legionnaire could be as insulting as he pleased — when he, Captain Herman Sturmer, wished to silence the fellow's tongue, he need only lift his hand. His *partizans* would do the work for him. Butcher? No, a soldier. He left the butchering to others.

His thin voice snapped harshly, 'Your brother needn't have died, Davidson. He was a brave soldier, and I respect brave soldiers. He came out of that pit where

172

the prisoners were kept and I told him not to go back. I said, 'Stay here until morning'. I think he knew what was going to happen, but he just said, 'My place is with my men, and he went back into the Pit of Hell, as journalists have since called it.'

It didn't worry him what the world thought of that action. At the time it had seemed the best tactical thing to do. It hadn't saved the defeated German African Army, but it had at least denied the advancing Allies the use of a thousand more men to harass the retreating Germans, trying to get out of Africa.

Sturmer reflected back to that time. The place wasn't far from here — rather nearer the coast, that was all. Scrub soil rather than sand, with rocky escarpments high to the east of them.

The prisoners had been confined in a steep-walled pocket in the rocky ground, from which there was just one difficult path leading out. It had been a good prison compound, requiring the minimum of guards to keep the prisoners in subjection.

But when the time had come for the Germans to retreat still further — retreat even across the sea — and there was no time to ship the prisoners with them, Sturmer had made his decision.

'You ran trucks up to the edge of the pit,' Tex said, his words harsh because his brother had walked back to die with his men. 'You had rubber pipes dangling from their exhausts, an' durin' the night you left the trucks runnin', didn't you?'

Sturmer's hand was lifting. He had a short temper and refused to have his dignity assailed any further. Tex saw the action and knew what it meant. That gun was still too far out of reach. He was going out, and he didn't have a chance to defend himself, save with his fists, and they weren't any good against men armed with swords and guns.

So he shouted the truth. 'You killed half the men while they slept. You filled that pit with exhaust gases an' poisoned 'em so they never woke again. But some of the men woke — '

That hand paused. The owner saw a chance of cruelty. 'One was your brother?'

'They tried to get out of the pit, up that steep, winding pathway.' He had been, had seen it, on his return to Africa a year ago. That was when a newspaper in America published a story that there was a Captain Sturmer in the French Foreign Legion, and it was whispered that it was the former Nazi General Sturmer, who had disappeared with the collapse of Germany at the war-end. Tex had come over to find out for himself if it was true. And there was no mistaking it, this was the same Sturmer.

'They were shot down by machine-gunners,' said Sturmer coldly. 'If they had been sensible, they could have died in their beds.' His eyes flickered behind those glasses. 'Your brother was the first to die. He was right in front of those men. We trained the searchlights on them, and then kept the guns running. It was all over in an hour.'

Then his hand started to go up again.

9

A *partizan* shouted, his voice crackling like a whiplash. Everyone wheeled, scenting danger.

A lone Arab stood almost in their midst. He had walked in towards them while *partizans* and officer were engrossed with their prisoner.

A *partizan* said something, his voice harsh in the silence. The oncoming Arab just shuffled nearer, without looking up. Tex was looking at the white-robed figure, and manoeuvring his horse at the same time.

Then the Arab lifted his head. Tex saw a flat, battered brown face, a nose squashed between the high cheekbones. Blue eyes.

No Arab . . .

Elegant!

Grim-faced, the Legionnaire from Brooklyn, flung open his burnous and started to bring up the rifle hidden there.

It caught. Tex saw the look of horror on Elegant's face as he struggled to get the gun levelled. The *partizans* were shouting and wheeling their horses at the sight of danger. Then one ran into Elegant and knocked him flying. The rifle crashed into the sand and lay part-buried.

Tex saw Elegant's face. It had been a gallant, desperate bid to save a comrade, and it had failed. Now despair was written on that homely, battered mug of Legionnaire Ellighan.

Tex heard a sharp, barked order from Sturmer. At once the *partizans* wheeled away, though they put down their terrible *flissas* with reluctance. They liked to do the killing — not their officer.

For Sturmer, infuriated by the angry, insolent words of the tall American, intended to kill the brash intruder in the Arab disguise.

Tex was that much nearer now . . .

Sturmer's hand started to go down towards his gun. Tex's hand, trained to a lightning draw, flashed out and beat him to it — beat him by minutes, or so it seemed, so fast was that draw.

Sturmer felt the barrel slam into his ribs; startled, he looked into a face with grim, grey eyes, a mouth that was as hard as any mouth could be.

'Get them hands up,' grated the ex-cowpuncher. 'Right up. An' tell them mavericks o' yourn to stand back or I'll sure punch holes through your body with this gun!'

The *partizans* didn't need to be told, however. They saw that fiercely determined American face, saw the gun slammed so hard into their officer's body that he was pulling away from it in pain and they kept back, circling watchfully, hands on guns, ready to open fire at the first opportunity.

Tex bellowed to Elegant. 'Get your gun, brother, an' fix yourself a hoss.'

Elegant came stumbling across, trying to shake the sand out of his rifle barrel. A grin of relief was coming to his face but nearness to death had left the Brooklyn man shaken and he looked sickly. But he was recovering.

He wanted to take Sturmer's horse, because that magnificent beast was clearly the best there, but Tex stopped him. 'Sturmer goes back with us — right to America, if we can take him.'

Legionnaire Ellighan looked uneasily at the *partizans*. He didn't want to get any nearer to those fierce-faced men. Tex heard him whisper, 'We saw you . . . We're hid up back of that hill in front of you. This was Rube's idea . . . '

Sure, it would be Rube who got the ideas. A daring, hazardous plan which had failed, yet in the end had succeeded in its objective. And it would be like Elegant, Tex's special buddy in the Legion, to insist on trying to put it across.

Tex saw those worried blue eyes looking up at him. This altered things, to find that the rest of the party was so near. For the others rode camels . . .

Elegant whispered, 'What are we gonna do? About them buzzards?' He nodded towards the *partizans*, ready to pounce.

Tex just said, 'Call 'em up — I mean Rube and the others. The *partizans* won't touch us while this gun's ticklin' their boss's ribs. He's goin' with us.'

Elegant didn't get it. He shook his big

head under the Arab headdress but did as he was told. He turned towards the north and spread his arms wide above his head. In a few minutes they saw the camels come lurching into view around a rolling mound of wind-scoured sand.

Sturmer never moved. He couldn't, not safely, with that grim-faced man leaning on a revolver pressed hard into his side. He didn't say anything either, but his looks were poisonous. Bitterly now he was regretting his failure to decapitate Legionnaire Hank Davidson on sight. But then there were things he wanted to know about the man with the familiar face.

The Legionnaire from Brooklyn was stripping off his Arab clothing. He wore his uniform complete underneath.

'Abdul's?' Tex asked, his eyes watching that advancing party. They were looking for Nicky Shaw, American newspaperwoman, who had no right to be there. He couldn't see her on the camels.

'You mean that wounded Arab?' Elegant nodded. He asked, 'What happened to the post? We saw the place go up in flames? Who did it?'

'Ay-rabs,' said Tex laconically. Then he frowned. He still couldn't see Nicky. Just a couple walking by the side of the camels and three up on the swaying humps — three men.

Elegant nodded. 'That's what we thought. So we sat down to watch what happened. We figger if maybe you'd get kept behind.'

'I must have passed you in the dark — just.' That had turned out to be a fortunate circumstance. Tex glanced across at the *partizans*. They had grouped together. They were plotting something. He didn't know what it was, but he was uneasy. Those twelve renegade Arabs were dangerous — very dangerous.

His eyes flickered back to the advancing party. He stiffened. Nicky wasn't . . .

She was. He found a sigh of relief escaping him. He didn't want to think of harm coming to the girl, and for a moment he'd feared the worst.

Nicky was walking. She'd probably had enough of camel riding in the past days, anyway. She had changed into blouse and slacks, and because of her men's pants,

Tex had failed to recognize her.

She had her camera out, and as she came up she kept halting, kept lifting it to her eye and photographing the scene. She looked very fresh and attractive in that clean, white blouse. Tex saw then that Elegant and Rube were looking at her, and knew she looked attractive to them, too.

As she came right up to the two mounted men she called, 'Let's see that gun a bit more, Tex. Boy, is this some picture! When New York gets this — '

Tex said, dryly, 'You think they ever will?' But the girl went on opening her shutter on the scene until Tex had to put a stop to it.

Rube gave him the glad 'Hi, bub!' from on top a camel as they lurched level. Tex shouted, 'Keep goin', Rube. Next stop Lake Chad!' He prodded Sturmer so that the ex-Nazi gasped. 'Here's our ticket I guess.' A ticket that gave immediate safety, anyway.

Dimmy was walking with Nicky, dutifully carrying her precious photographic instruments. He gave a big, inane grin when he saw Tex but couldn't think of anything to say at such short notice.

Louie was standing on the neck of the last camel. Tex looked into a face black with worry. He saw those loose lips pulled back, showing the long, yellow teeth within, and thought how appropriately Louie the Camel had been nick-named. Except that no camel looked as filled with anxiety as Louie at that moment.

Louie came up, his eyes trying to look at Sturmer and the nearby *partizans* at the same time. He was a very unhappy man. Plainly he thought they had walked into a death trap and he was a mass of nerves.

As he drew level, he spoke quickly, and Tex saw that his brown, anxious eyes were looking straight at Sturmer. 'I didn't want to come. They made me — with a gun. I'd have stayed back at the post, I tell you.'

Tex grunted contemptuously. Louie was trying to make the grade with Sturmer in case the *partizan* chief turned the tables on the Legionnaires.

Bur all he said aloud, was, 'You'd be

dead by now, if you had, Louie. The Ay-rabs came an' killed nigh on every man at the post, then set fire to the place.'

The young, bearded Arab was on a camel beyond Louie. He smiled slightly at Tex and nodded, and the Texan knew that that was his thanks. Elegant rolled the burnous into a ball and tossed it up to the Arab who dressed himself, then Tex told him to get up behind Captain Sturner and hold that revolver pressed into the man's back. That was safer and more comfortable than trying to ride alongside and cover him at the same time, he'd found.

Rube kept going, leading the party southwards as if the distance to British territory was a mere day's ride, instead of over a thousand miles. It would take weeks, but Rube wasn't worried about that. So long as he was out of that damn' Legion he didn't care if it took years.

Nicky swung up on her camel and pulled it alongside Tex. She seemed to have learned quite a bit about camel handling in the weeks she had been in the country, and was quite at home, perched up on that hump.

She grinned at Tex. She looked the real McCoy, Tex thought, and was proud to be of the same race as this cheerful, unafraid, blue-eyed American girl.

'Brother,' he heard her say, 'you're the man for my money every time, I kept saying, no one'll keep you from catching up with us, and I was right. Tell me how you did it.'

Tex said, 'I just whistled up a thousand Ay-rabs an' they dug me out.' He glanced back.

The *partizans* had fallen into procession no more than fifty yards behind them. It made his scalp rise, because those men were armed and if they wished they could shoot them out of their saddles any time they chose. The only thing was they didn't want to see their officer killed. Herman Sturmer was a great one for finding deserters, and he brought much in bounty money for the renegades — money — and savage thrills.

Tex didn't say anything to the girl. She'd find out soon enough, anyway. There wasn't a thing he could do about it so he kept them walking along at the same leisurely camel pace that was yet hard to keep up with on foot.

He told what had happened at the fort, and then the girl gave their story. 'It worked like a charm,' she said. 'We went out dressed as camel men, taking the water to the beasts. We saw Elly, Rube, and the others come on guard, and then, just when it was almost dark, we came out from hiding and introduced our-selves. We started off almost immediately, scattering the other camels, and — well, you know the rest.'

'How's Abdul?' Tex's eyes went up to that hunched white figure immediately ahead of Louie now.

Nicky said, 'It isn't Abdul. It's 'brahim-ibn-something — I can't remember. He's getting well rapidly now, but weak still, I guess.'

''brahim?' repeated Tex. 'You're sure gettin' on well with the Ay-rab, by the sound of things.'

Nicky retorted, 'Why not? I always did like men with beards. They kinda thrill simple New York girls, I guess.' She fluffed her fair hair. 'I might tell you, brother, 'brahim's proposed marriage every mile of the last ten we've covered!'

'The heck he has,' exclaimed Tex. 'I didn't help rescue him to compete in the blonde market. What's he got to offer that I ain't got?' If she could make a joke about it, so could he.

'He's son of a minor chieftain hereabouts, he told me. Says his father has plenty of goats, plenty of camels, and so many wives it sounds scandalous.' Demurely she kept her eyes away from Tex's. 'He says if I marry him, he won't have any other wives. Not for a long time, anyway.'

So Tex said, 'It's a fair bargain, honey. You take him up on that. Mind you, livin' among goats an' camels sure plays hell with the nostrils after fifteen or twenty years. Maybe, after all, New York's not such a bad place to find a husband in . . . or Texas.'

'Now Texas, that's a place I've always wanted to visit,' she said thoughtfully.

The Brooklyn bouncer was listening, sitting closer to the silent frigid Sturmer

187

than that officer's own shadow. He looked eagerly across at the laughing girl, his flattened features ashine with enthusiasm.

'You wanna visit Brooklyn sometime. We got a bridge. You ain't never seen a bridge till you see ours, I guess. You come an' I'll take you every yard of the way across an' tell you all about it,' he said cunningly. Elegant was smitten but his technique wasn't so good.

Louie got an eyeful of *partizans* right at that moment. His stomach probably somersaulted at seeing those white-hooded, sinister figures riding so silently. so closely upon their heels. He shouted to his camel and tapped it with the barrel of his Lebel and turned it closer in towards the party.

He had the jitters badly. His frightened eyes stared at Captain Sturmer, and his long, yellow teeth showed again as he called, 'I didn't want to come on pump. They shoved a gun in my face an' said I didn't have a chance.'

Tex called, 'Okay, Louie. Sturmer heard you. He'll maybe treat you well if he gets away from us. Maybe . . . ' He didn't think so. Louie had come without much argument, they all knew, in spite of his protestations. Louie started to drop back. He was watching those *partizans* with an unhappy eye; plainly he feared them far more than the possible wrath of his comrades.

Elegant, pistol still hard in the captain's back, turned and yapped confidentially to Tex, 'The guy don't know what he's sayin'. He got his chance. We said, 'You goin' on pump, or do we knock you cold?' We gave him time to think it over — 'bout half a second it was — but he didn't need all that time an' he said he'd come.'

He was kidding the Bronx boy, and Louie couldn't take it. 'It's a Goddam lie,' he shouted. His eyes were anxiously upon the face of Sturmer, desperate in case he believed Ellighan. He kept on yammering, but no one took much notice of him, because he was a craven and this desert was no place for such men.

When Louie had dropped out of earshot, Tex said softly, 'I don't trust that guy, Elly. He's got himself so worked up, I figger he might do anythin' crazy.' He got his Lebel round. He'd hate to do it, but if Louie started anything, he'd put a stop to his game. Their lives were as valuable as his . . .

Elly wrinkled his battered pan confidentially. 'That comes of being born in Bronx,' he yapped. 'Don't give you no sand, I reckon. Now Brooklyn . . . ' He was off on his favourite subject.

In the heat of the day they stopped for a couple of hours in the shadow thrown by a tall rock formation that had been a beacon to them all morning. The *partizans* dismounted in a flurry of once-white robes and ate their repast and watched from a distance even less than fifty yards now. But they wouldn't do anything while that revolver was stuck in the middle of Sturmer's back.

Tex said each in turn would have to watch the prisoner, even the wounded Arab. He was strong enough now to use a gun, anyway, and had quickly volunteered when he heard them discussing duty turns. Sturmer had his hands tied in front of him, to make sure he didn't surprise the guard.

Then they all drank briefly from their bottles, though they could have drunk the lot and more, too, ate some hard, black, Arab bread, and then stretched out to catch up with the sleep they had lost during the night.

Close by them the *partizans* lay down and watched or slept.

When they resumed their journey, the twelve white-robed figures mounted and silently jogged after them.

Nicky said, 'If this is going on all the way to Lake Chad, I'll go screwy, Tex.' She looked round at the sinister figures, shuddered and turned her eyes away quickly. 'It's getting me down,' she whispered.

It was getting them all down. At first they had expected the *partizans* to get tired and in time sheer off, but after a while it began to dawn on them that their enemies had no intention of leaving them while their officer was in their hands.

All began to suffer from nerves, with those figures so close upon their heels, just waiting for a fatal slip on their part.

'God, give 'em half a chance to rescue

Sturmer an' we'd be for it,' Tex thought. This time there'd be no dilly-dallying, he decided grimly, looking at that pale-faced, cold-looking ex-Nazi officer beside them. Just give him a chance, and he'd have his *partizans*' swords whistling around their ears in no time. Their heads would be off in a second.

'We mustn't give 'em even half a chance,' he reflected. He kept telling himself there was nothing to worry about. Just keep that revolver slammed into Sturmer's ribs so that he had no chance to escape, and the *partizans* could follow them up to their necks in Lake Chad, for all it could hurt them.

Yet even Tex kept worrying.

All that afternoon the little procession wound its way among the sand dunes on the way south. They were so tired from their night's exertions, so saturated with the heat of that awful, burning sun, that for hours on end they rode with scarcely a word spoken between them.

When evening came, and a cool wind began to spring up off the desert, they relaxed and recovered their spirits a little and even talked. Then Tex got Nicky's story from her.

She'd been in Algiers, writing up stories, about Arab nationalism for her editor back in New York. 'I take pictures too,' she said. 'Maybe that old sourpuss of an editor of mine remembered I do two jobs for one pay check, for suddenly he sent me a cable.'

'Try to find Sturmer?' Tex guessed.

'Sure. The story kept popping up in the American Press that General Herman Sturmer had joined the Foreign Legion, but no one knew for certain. The Legion H.Q. in France wouldn't say a thing . . . '

'They never do, about their recruits,' Tex said. 'That's policy. Not even war criminals. I guess the Legion's stiff with 'em, anyway.'

So Nicky had paid out large amounts of good American dollars, and because of her sympathetic articles on Arab national-ism, she had been allowed to travel secretly with caravans crossing that part of the desert said to be patrolled by Sturmer and his *partizans*. She'd about given up hope of ever meeting the man, when suddenly he had turned up. The only thing was, this was the only time they had found a wounded Arab wandering in the desert and taken him in. That action could have cost them plenty if Sturmer had found him in the train.

' 'brahim sure caused us some trouble,' sighed Tex. He shuddered, thinking of the narrow escapes they'd had in consequence of trying to help the wounded man.

Nicky said, 'That fellow's grateful, though, Tex. He sure thinks you're a mighty fine man.'

Tex said. 'Goldarn it, Nicky, he sure ought to.'

Then came the problem of camping for the night. Tex picked a small mound upon which the whole party could rest. They had no means of making a fire, because they were off the caravan routes upon which could be found dried dung, and this meant an anxious vigil for the watchers, who had to sit up and try to see movement against the starry, night sky. The moon came up about midnight, however, and after that there was less for them to worry about.

As it was, for all their trepidation, just nothing happened all during the night. For all the sounds they heard, the *partizans* might have cleared off.

They hadn't, however. When they stirred at dawn they looked round. As the light strengthened they saw a string of white figures completely surrounding that little hillock. The *partizans* hadn't taken any chances on their escape under cover of darkness.

When Tex led the way down off that sand dune, the silent, fierce-eyed Arab renegades gave way to them reluctantly. The *partizans* went back no more than twenty yards from them and watched as the equally silent Sturmer was ridden through.

Then they fell in right behind the last camel and rode in their dust all the day. This time it really worked on their nerves, and even Dimmy sensed the threatening atmosphere and didn't like it. It made the men quarrelsome, and Louie kept picking on Dimmy, and then Rube and Elegant picked on him.

Once again, Nicky, no longer bright and confident, whispered, 'Gosh. Tex, isn't there anything we can do to get rid of 'em?'

'Like turn an' start shootin'?' He was cynical. He had seen enough gun-play and knew how many got hurt. 'They'd open fire then, if we started on them,' he told her. 'Even if we drove them off — killed 'em all — it wouldn't be before they'd hit some of us. Okay, sister, you tell me which of us they'd hit?'

She shrugged. There wasn't an answer to that question.

So Tex said, softly, 'Honey, it might be you, and I wouldn't want that to happen.'

She said nothing at that, and they rode for the next ten miles in silence. In the middle of the afternoon they almost ran into a party of Arabs,

It was a fast-riding bunch, working their way northwards. There were a good fifty horsemen, and the men in blue tunics didn't relish the idea of meeting so many traditional Legion enemies.

Tex gave the order to dismount out of sight. When he looked behind he couldn't see the *partizans*. They didn't want to meet any of their kind, either, and they'd gone for cover. But he knew they hadn't left them; for there was no rising cloud of dust to their rear, to tell of fast-running horses.

Then they stood and watched that fast-moving bunch of Arabs. When they were about a mile away and seemingly heading straight towards them, the leaders suddenly veered and started off up a long, wide, sandy valley. In another five minutes they would be out of sight and he and his party could safely mount and continue their way.

Safely? He looked back cynically to where he knew the *partizans* were. There'd be no safety for them while that bunch was on their tracks.

He saw an Arab renegade come riding his horse into view. They weren't going to be left behind while their officer and master was a prisoner . . . besides, the heads of five *poumpists* would bring them each a couple of month's pay in bounty.

Tex saw the beautiful cream-coffee coloured stallion of Sturmer's sidle away, as if someone was mounting on the far side. Then he caught a glimpse of an Arab headdress . . . His Lebel came leaping up, then lowered as 'brahim, the wounded Arab's face showed above the saddle. Then he shouted, because 'brahim was painfully pulling himself up on to the horse's back.

At the shout, 'brahim sent the beautiful horse leaping away, pulling himself into the saddle as he did so. 'brahim waved and shouted something in Arabic and then headed after the receding Arabs, now a mile and a half away.

There was consternation among the Legionnaires. They didn't know what to do. They had grown to like the young Arab, and couldn't find it in themselves to shoot him down, though he was running away with their best horse. Besides, to fire would have attracted attention from the Arabs, who might have returned to investigate the shooting.

Tex shrugged and called, 'Let him go.' They had enough enemies, without bringing more on to them. But it made him cynical to see the young Arab go off on that fine horse. They had risked enough to help the man, and now — this.

The *partizans* were all mounted and watching silently from about thirty yards away. Tex called ironically, 'Time to go, fellars. The guard of honour's paradin'.'

This time Sturmer had to ride a camel. Elegant sat on the hump, with the ex-Nazi standing on the thick, trunk-like neck. Sturmer lost his temper at the prospect of riding a camel, and he shouted abuse in German. He couldn't understand yet, his position, and was demanding the horse that Tex was riding. Tex said, 'Not on your life, fellar,' and that was that.

They started again, plodding steadily southwards. A fresh worry came to Tex, soon after starting. They were nearly out of water and had been depending on 'brahim to lead them to a waterhole. He'd promised to do that, and had said it was a few hours' ride ahead. But without him for a guide, they were pretty sure to miss the place in this vast land of sand.

That wasn't a good prospect, to be wandering in the middle of the Sahara without water. But it was facing them.

About five in the afternoon, after three intolerable hours in the saddle, he gave the weary party the order to halt for a short rest. He wanted to do another ten miles before darkness, but he knew they must have a rest.

Elegant had played watchdog long enough. He handed his revolver to Tex, who put Sturmer in charge of the other men. Each would take it in turns to rest and watch the prisoner. Then they ate as much as their parched mouths would take, and finished off their precious water supply. It amounted to little more than a mouthful each. That meant they had to find water before darkness.

In spite of their anxiety, the party dozed. They were without shade, lying there at the mouth of a dry wadi, and their discomfort seemed about as great as when they were travelling. But still it rested them a little, and the camels, at any rate, needed a halt.

Nicky had dropped by Tex's side. Neither spoke but they lay and looked at each other until they fell asleep. Nicky was looking drawn; her blouse was soiled

200

and she wasn't the immaculate figure of two days before. Yet still she had courage; still she could smile gallantly at the big Legionnaire.

Tex went to sleep wearily, wondering if there hadn't been better plans than to come heading straight across the mighty Sahara. It was all very well for Rube to argue that thousands of Arabs crossed safely every year. They just weren't Ay-rabs, he thought . . .

Someone was talking. He wished they wouldn't. In his half-sleep he tried to imagine where anyone found the strength to talk . . . Sturmer's voice . . . Sturmer? He'd hardly spoken since his capture . . .

Louie's voice. Now what was Louie doing, whispering to Sturmer?

It should have been a warning to Tex, but his sun-drugged, weary mind reacted slowly to the hint of danger. Yet, in time, he dragged himself on to his arm and peered through almost closed eyes in the direction where he had last seen Sturmer.

Sturmer had gone!

An Arab was there in his place.

A partizan!

10

Tex saw that fierce face, with its ragged goat beard under the turbanned head. Saw the Legion-issue Lebel jump up to cover him . . .

Saw that Louie the Camel was missing, and then saw him standing back towards the dismounted *partizans*, creeping in to attack. Sturmer was gesticulating . . . demanding a gun. Louie was biting his nails off as the headhunters came round him.

Tex rolled. He shouted. And he drew his gun faster than he'd ever drawn a Colt before. It leapt into his hand as he rolled to his knees. It splashed flame before that brown renegade finger could tighten on the Lebel trigger. And he killed the *partizan* a fraction of a second before the Arab tried to kill him.

Nicky started to rise, and Tex threw her in between the narrow walls of the wadi. Rube came plunging up, Lebel firing from the hip. Elegant ran towards the

202

camels, heard lead whistling and saw the beasts go prancing away, and dived for cover behind a sand dune instead.

Dimmy got hit and lay where he was. Tex emptied his revolver, sending the surprised *partizans* into cover. Louie and Sturmer went with them. Then there was a curious silence, with everybody keeping his head down for a few minutes.

Tex was in a rage at being tricked. He shouted, 'Louie you're a goddamn' heel. You keep outa my sight after this, or by God I'll not be responsible for what I do to you.'

Nicky was lying quivering by his side, not quite realizing how the tables had been turned on them.

Tex said, savagely, 'I should have known. Louie always was a heel. But I didn't think a fellar could get as low as this, sellin' us to the enemy.'

'To save his own skin,' Nicky nodded. 'He's been terrified of the *partizans* ever since they got on our trail . . . '

Tex snarled, 'Wal, that guy won't get no change outa Sturmer. The hell, Sturmer won't remember what he did for him;

he'll have his head off in no time.'

He stopped. Elegant's voice drifted over from behind that dune. 'Louie, you didn't oughta do that,' he complained. Curious, even now Elegant couldn't get angry with the Camel, was only mildly chiding. 'You got an inferiority complex, I keep tellin' you, Louie. That's what makes you do things like this. You oughta bin born in Brooklyn. You don't have time to get no complexes there, I reckon.'

That plaintive, yapping Brooklyn voice kept on for a long time, but it brought no answer from the Camel. Then Tex, watching now over a ragged stone outcrop that was burning hot to the touch, saw a swift, white movement beyond and opened fire. The Arab tumbled out of sight, but Tex didn't know whether he'd been hit or not. He wished he had a Lebel. A revolver was all right for work at close quarters, but against this creeping enemy, the more precise rifle was better.

Elegant blazed away a couple of quick rounds, and there was an immediate, furious return of fire from the *partizans*.

A high-pitched scream told of a hit. Then there was silence again, while the descending sun blazed mercilessly upon their backs, and the bright yellow sand hills reflected light at them and made them gasp for breath. The heat was intolerable, but they couldn't escape it.

Far worse, though, was the torture of thirst. That last mouthful hadn't assuaged their raging thirst, and now they were in torment for lack of water.

Tex heard Nicky whisper hoarsely, 'My tongue's so dry, Tex, I can hear it rattling in my head.'

He told her, 'Don't talk — an' keep your head down.' And then he tried to figure out a way of escape from this situation.

They had lost their camels; they were without water and didn't know where the nearest waterhole was. They were being attacked by a vicious enemy, and were outnumbered by at least four to one.

Tex thought, 'I've been in healthier places.'

He saw another movement, and snapped off with the last round in his revolver. He put his hand into his pocket for a reload. There was nothing there. He'd had a few loose rounds taken from Sturmer, but they must have dropped out of his pocket during the scramble for cover.

Looking back towards where he had lain he saw sunlight glinting on brass, but that was the only round he could see. The rest were probably buried in the sand.

He didn't tell Nicky. Rube pumped away for the first time, and then they all crouched as a ragged cloud of lead came hissing balefully through the air above them. One came lower than the rest and sprayed them with hot sand.

Rube called, 'Watch out, Elly. They're closin' in on you.'

Almost they could imagine that flat face spitting in contempt. 'They ain't gonna get the better of a kid from Brooklyn,' he yapped, and then, unexpectedly even for Tex and Rube, he came leaping towards the wadi in which they were crouching.

As he came diving in, he was firing from the hip. They saw him leaping, saw the snarl on his big, homely mug. Then he flopped beside them as more lead came zipping viciously towards him. They thought he had been hit, but when they turned to help him, he lifted his head and grinned and they were reassured.

Tex asked, 'Could you see Louie the rat?'

Elegant had got one glimpse of him. 'They've put him way back with their hosses. He's got a coupla *partizans* for company, an' I guess right now he don't feel so good.' He wormed his way alongside them, his body making a long trough in the soft sand. He shoved his rifle up and then they heard him say, 'From now on, I guess I ain't never gonna trust a guy that comes from the Bronx. They ain't nice.'

It was an epitaph on a friendship that had always been one-sided.

There was no more firing from the attackers after that. Risking a quick look over the ragged, stone outcrop before him, Tex saw a little group standing back a hundred yards or so where the horses were. One was Sturmer. Another, Louie. Louie was telling them something. Tex grabbed Rube's rifle and crashed shot after shot into the group and sent them all diving for cover.

Still there was no more firing from the *partizans*. After a while, Tex understood.

'Louie's told 'em we're out of water. Sturmer figures he need only sit aroun' an' wait for us to die — or give in.'

Rube said cynically, 'What's the difference?'

Elegant shook his big battered head and said, 'That Louie, I get so I don't like him at all.'

The waiting was trying. In another couple of hours the sun would be set, and then it would be cool, but what good would that do to them? It wouldn't stop this intolerable thirst — only water could do that, and they wouldn't find any in the darkness.

There'd be no getting away from this spot, either, now, they all knew. This time they hadn't a hostage to give them immunity from attack, and they couldn't get far without horses or camels in this arid land.

'They'll just lie aroun' all night,' Tex

thought. 'They won't bother even to attack us. They know tomorrow's sun will put an end to us.'

He squinted over the top again, and wondered what sort of an end it would be. Would they just lie there and gradually weaken with thirst, until unconsciousness came to them and they were at the mercy of their enemies? Or would they go fighting mad and use the last remnants of their strength in a futile attack on the *partizans*, knowing they must die but being determined to take others with them?

He knew without being told what end he would choose. He'd always been a fighter, always had had to be. But that didn't solve the problem of Nicky. Walking out and dying would leave the girl at the mercy of these merciless enemies. He thought, 'Better see she gets a bullet first.' Sturmer would never allow her to live, and it was like the man to hand her over to these vicious renegades of his.

It made him feel sick inside, but Tex thought again. 'Better save a bullet for her . . . '

When he looked at her, she was lying on her side, her eyes nearly closed but looking at him, all the same. They opened a little more when she saw his eyes upon her. Her voice was a croak of sound now, but somehow she managed to make it sound cheerful.

'What was the fighting Texan thinking just then? You should have seen your face, Tex,' she said softly. 'It was . . . ruthless.'

Tex said, 'It was somethin' I was havin' to think about. Somethin' I wouldn't want to do.' But he didn't tell her what.

She whispered, 'Isn't there any hope, Tex?'

He shrugged. 'There's always a hope, Nicky, but just now — wal, you figger out our chances for yourself. Which is gonna win? Thirst — or death from a bullet?'

She sighed. 'I never expected it to turn out like this. It was all a gay adventure, setting off on that assignment to get Sturmer's picture.'

Tex said, 'We never figger things are gonna turn out as they do. But — keep your chin up, honey. We're not dead yet.'

She reached out and stroked his bare

arm, smoothing out the soft silky hairs upon it. There was affection in that gesture. She said, 'Tex, I'm not sorry I met you. I mean, not even now. You're a mighty fine man, and I'm proud to know you.'

Tex cracked, 'Honey, you say all that when we get back to America an' I can use that phone number of yours.' It made her laugh, and the sound, floating across the sand to the hidden *partizans*, must have puzzled them and perhaps set them to worrying.

Rube growled, 'I don't see what there is to laugh at.'

And then Elegant chipped in — 'Why don't you figger up a nice, bright scheme to get us outa this hole, Schemer? Remember, it was your idea to travel south! We won't meet no enemies that way, you said.'

Rube couldn't answer. His eyes forlornly peered over the sandy hill in front of him and he couldn't think of a way out of their situation.

There wasn't a way, of course, he was thinking desperately. The odds were piled a yard high against them. He lost his temper and raved at Louie.

'Blast you for a traitor,' he shouted. 'Come out an' let me kill you!'

But Louie didn't take up the invitation, and it only served to reassure their enemies, left wondering by Nicky's disconcerting laughter. From Rube's tone, it must have been apparent how desperate the defenders were now.

Another half hour to sunset. Their thirst was like a raging fire that suffused their veins throughout the whole of their bodies. It affected their vision too. They found their eyelids were getting gummed together, and they had difficulty in focusing.

Then they started to imagine things. That the *partizans* were moving, were closing in for the kill. When they concentrated, however, they realized it was just an hallucination, caused by shimmering air currents rising from the burning hot sand and distorting images.

Then Tex began to think that Dimmy was moving.

He dismissed the thought, so sure had

they all been that the silent Legionnaire was dead. But when he looked again he saw that Dimmy's hands were moving in little, ineffectual gestures, as if, in his semi-consciousness, he was trying to grasp something.

Dimmy was lying close up among a lot of little hillocks of sand that almost screened him from the Legionnaires. Tex kept looking and then he whispered, 'Nicky, see if your eyes are better than mine.'

Nicky wriggled up alongside him and peeped over the ragged rock that toothed up out of the sand. She saw what he was looking at, and promptly said, 'He's alive, Tex. Oh, what are we going to do?'

Tex looked at the sun, then back at Dimmy. He said, 'We can't leave him there, that's certain. He'll die without attention . . . ' His words ended hope-lessly. It looked as though Dimmy would die, anyway.

All the same, he couldn't see his comrade left to lie out there. He had to get him in among them. Their desperate plight made Tex so reckless that he didn't count the risk anyway.

Before Nicky knew what he was up to, Tex had started to worm his way along the sand towards the stirring Legionnaire. Tex heard Nicky's sharp cry of horror as she saw him deliberately heading towards the *partizan* headhunters, but he went on. Then Nicky said something to Rube, and he heard bolts click back. Rube and the Brooklyn kid were standing by to cover him with rifle fire in case of need.

He hoped he wouldn't need it. Stuck out there he wouldn't stand much chance if the battle flared up again.

It took him a long time to get to Dimmy's side. For one thing, he had to proceed with the utmost caution, snaking on his stomach the whole of the way, seeking every little undulation in the ground that would give him cover. Another thing, hours in that torrid heat without water had drained the strength from him.

It seemed to Tex that the journey over that hot sand would never come to an end. It seemed miles, a relentless, never-ending drag that left his shoulder muscles sore from the effort of having to pull himself through the soft, yielding sand. There was sweat in his eyes, and a salt taste in his mouth. He was panting open-mouthed now, like an overworked dog, and the dust got into his throat and made the agony of thirst just so much worse.

He kept thinking of water as he grimly ploughed to the rescue of his stricken comrade — long cold draughts of water with ice clinking in it; jugs of water, barrels of water, whole darned lakes of water! He couldn't keep his thoughts off the subject.

He tried to think of El Kwatra and the fate of his comrades there. He wondered what had happened to Ca-ca and his traitor friends — by now they were probably riding comfortably, under Arab escort, towards some seaport where native fishermen would give them passage across to Europe. The Arabs, he was pretty sure, would keep their side of the bargain, whatever their thoughts of the wretched traitors.

He was too far gone to work up anger

now at the treachery of the men, and not even Louie's appalling conduct bothered him. Louie was just a man who had lost his nerve, that was all. It happened to all weak men who were pushed beyond breaking point. Tex found himself, in his tiredness, becoming even philosophical.

Then he came out within ten yards of Dimmy's feet.

And he found he had crawled into a trap!

Sturmer was crouched between two dunes, waiting for someone to come out and rescue poor Dimmy. They must have seen those twitching movements of the injured man's limbs, but cunningly hadn't attempted to finish him off — rather they had known that, once seen by the Legionnaires, his comrades would at all costs try to help him.

Gasping, peering through sweat-dimmed eyes, his face a white mask of desert dust that clung thickly to his brows and eyelashes, Tex saw three or four Arabs in hiding on either side of their leader. All had rifles trained on the Legionnaire from Texas. And Tex was unarmed, now that

216

his revolver was empty. So he gave in then, or appeared to do so. Now that he was discovered there was no need for him to go crawling on his face anymore. He sat up. Right at his feet something glittered brassily. One of the fallen rounds. But he couldn't reach out, couldn't very well slip it into the breach of the revolver. Not with those fierce-eyed Arabs and the malevolently triumphant Sturmer watching him.

Tex heard the gasp that came from his comrades in hiding, when he sat up. For a second they could not understand it. Tiredly he rubbed the dust out of his eyes and then stood up and called out. 'They've got me. You stay where you are, though.'

While there was life there was hope, he told himself even then. Precious little hope for his comrades and Nicky, but a whole lot more than what he'd got, he thought grimly.

He was swaying with fatigue as he faced Sturmer, still crouching with his men between those dunes. He said, dully, 'Looks like the game's up — for me, huh?'

Sturmer's harsh, triumphant voice rang out then. 'The game's up — for all of you. One by one you'll fall into our hands.'

'And then?' Tex's eyes watched that thin, eye-glassed figure, so slight, so unformidable, yet so terrible to his enemies.

'Then — ' said Sturmer, and finished the sentence with a quick gesture as of cutting a throat. The action seemed to excite the dark, long-faced, fiery-eyed renegades alongside him, and they began to move. One must have lifted out of cover, and at once either Rube or Elegant snapped off a shot that tore a hole in the shoulder of the Arab's burnous.

That Arab came under cover again very quickly.

Tex was now in a mood where he couldn't care what happened. He walked across to Dimmy and examined him. He'd been shot more than once. There was a puncture through his shoulder that hadn't bled much because the hot sun had formed a protective clot of blood and that had acted like a bandage. There was also a nasty, long wound at the side of his head. Creased, was how Tex thought of it, looking down.

His eyes caught a brassy glint right up against the body of his comrade. Another of his lost rounds of ammunition.

He went down on his knee and examined Dimmy. He wasn't in a good way at all. Much longer exposed and he'd be past help.

Tex rose to his feet. He had to put his hand to the ground to do so, and when he stood upright once again that precious round was in his hand. That round was for Sturmer, if he had half a chance.

Sturmer was watching him, silently enjoying the moment. This time there could be no escape for this relentless American, who had followed him half-way across the world to effect retribution for that crime in the Pit of Hell. He felt he could afford to wait a few moments longer.

Tex looked at the man. 'What about the gal?' he demanded, his head jerking towards where Nicky was hidden with the other two Legionnaires.

Sturmer said, thinly, 'Tell your comrades to give themselves up and I'll see no harm comes to her.'

Tex looked at that face and knew the man was lying. Then his eyes flickered beyond, to the long shadows cast by this rolling waste of sand. He caught a glimpse of blue. Louie. He was still alive then. He was crouching with some other renegades, probably close to where the horses were hidden.

As his eyes trailed hopelessly back towards Sturmer, Tex caught another movement. There were Arabs farther west of them. He hadn't realized that Sturmer had so many followers; the Legionnaires couldn't have killed many — or any, it seemed.

Casually he let his hand go into his tunic pocket. That was where the empty revolver was. He began to reload it inside the pocket. Sturmer was over-confident, sure that his enemy was unarmed. He didn't say anything at sight of Tex with his hands dug deep into his pockets, standing there apparently considering what had been said to him.

Then Tex got the round in, got the safety catch off so that it could fire in an instant. He turned and shouted, 'Rube, see that Nicky doesn't fall into this swine's hands. It wouldn't be nice for her . . . '

Sturmer lost his temper again. '*Schwein?*' he rasped. 'You dog, you have lived long enough!'

Tex threw himself sideways and drew. The revolver stuck in his pocket. There was an explosion and the smell of scorched cloth. Tex shouted with fury. That precious cartridge, designed for the despatch of Sturmer, had been wasted because of the accident, after all.

And Tex, rolling in the sand, was unarmed again and at the mercy of his enemies. Sturmer was shouting, 'Kill him! Kill him!'

Someone else was shouting, too. 'brahim! His voice carried from a distance of a hundred yards or so — 'Down, Tex, down!'

Tex obeyed. Rolled and kept on rolling. Lead was smacking up clouds of dust. Rube and Elly were blazing off in a furious endeavour to protect him. But overhead enough lead was screaming to have come from a troop of infantry, almost.

Tex lifted his head because he just had to see what was happening. He saw a flood of Arabs storming across the yellow dunes, screaming their war-cries. *Allah-o-Akbar!*

He found himself thinking again. 'I never realized that Sturmer had so many men,' and then he understood.

For 'brahim was among these new attackers. 'brahim, riding up behind the foot warriors on that glorious, cream-coffee coloured stallion that had been Sturmer's.

'brahim had brought those fast-moving Arabs back to help his friends . . . or had he?

Tex took a chance and shouted the information to his comrades. Sturmer and his Arabs were fleeing towards where their horses were hidden. Some of the renegades stopped lead and went down or were overrun by Arabs who showed short shrift to the renegades.

Tex scrambled back behind the cover where Nicky and the Legionnaires were crouching. Nicky grabbed him and hugged him in delight. 'We thought you were a goner,' she said and somehow found tears in her desiccated frame to weep at the thought. Tex marvelled that a hardboiled newspaperwoman should cry, then put it down to the nerve-wracking experiences she had passed through.

He didn't take his arm from around her slim waist, for all that. Thirst or no thirst, heat or no heat, it was good to be holding her again.

They saw the fury of sudden battle, as the renegades mounted and turned on the Arabs on foot. Then the tide went forward again, because the attackers were in too great a force to be stopped by six or eight *partizans* — all that were left now of Sturmer's force.

Tex groaned, 'He'll get away yet!' Sturmer had found a horse. He wasn't waiting to help his men in the raging little battle among the sand dunes. Instead he thrashed it into speed and went northwards as hard as he could go.

A second later another horseman followed. It was Louie.

Three Arab renegades managed to get away; nine were left, dead or about to die, on the sands . . .

* * *

'brahim came over, smiling. Painfully he got down from his horse and held out his hand. The Legionnaires rose and took it, but they looked doubtfully at the other Arabs who were closing in on them. They didn't expect much mercy from strange Arabs.

'brahim said, 'These are the bodyguard of Abdul el Nuhas. He was on his way to join the rebels in the north. He has promised that no harm shall come to you because you saved my life.'

Elegant said, 'All I want now is a drink, brudder!'

Within a few seconds the quartet were in the centre of a throng of fierce-looking men who softened into smiles and slapped them on the back and said 'Americano' in delight. It was difficult to imagine in them the enemy so dreaded by the Legion . . .

Dimmy was attended to by an Arab physician who was accompanying the returning nationalist leader. His opinion was that Dimmy would suffer no great harm provided he was allowed time in which to rest and recover from his wounds.

'brahim said, smilingly, 'You will go to Bir Khula, an oasis which is my father's. You will stay there and rest until your comrade is well, and then Nuhas Pasha has promised you safe escort to the coast. I personally will go with you. Allah will reward you for saving my life,' he ended. He was a very grateful Arab, and their friend for life.

Tex slapped him on the shoulder, refreshed by the drink they had poured into him. They moved away. When Tex returned it was to tell his friends that camp was to be made where they were for the night, and tomorrow they would move on to the oasis with Dimmy.

It was a glorious night, no moon at first, but with stars shedding their twinkling radiance on earth. The four sat close together, soothed by the desert breeze that blew coolly now that darkness had fallen. Soon they would sleep. Meanwhile they wanted to keep awake, because they were still alive and they could hardly believe it. After all, they had won through. Now it was only a question of time before they reached the coast — and then America.

Nicky said, 'Oh Tex, we're gonna have a grand time at that oasis, forgetting the nightmare of the past few days.'

Tex said, absently, 'Sure, sure.'

But when they awoke in the morning, he'd gone with Abdul el Nuhas and his men.

Tex had come across the Atlantic to find Sturmer. Sturmer was still alive.

Tex wasn't going to leave North Africa without the ex-Nazi. This time, though, he would operate from the Arab lines . . .

THE END